Rafaello vented a husky laugh.

"What have you got to offer me in return?" he demanded.

"Undying gratitude?" Glory suggested, without much hope.

"Something for nothing is not my style. Perhaps you should appeal to my baser instincts. Let me think. What do *I* want that *you* can give me?" Rafaello rested dark deep-set eyes that were shimmering with glints of awakening on her taut seated figure. "Only one thing. *Sex*."

LYNNE GRAHAM was born in Northern Ireland and has been a keen Mills & Boon reader since her teens. She is very happily married, with an understanding husband who has learned to cook since she started to write! Her five children keep her on her toes. When time allows, Lynne is a keen gardener.

Books by Lynne Graham

HARLEQUIN PRESENTS®
2163—DAMIANO'S RETURN
2182—THE ARABIAN MISTRESS
2199—DUARTE'S CHILD

Lynne Graham

RAFAELLO'S MISTRESS

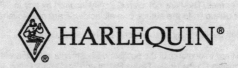

HARLEQUIN®

TORONTO • NEW YORK • LONDON
AMSTERDAM • PARIS • SYDNEY • HAMBURG
STOCKHOLM • ATHENS • TOKYO • MILAN • MADRID
PRAGUE • WARSAW • BUDAPEST • AUCKLAND

ISBN 0-373-12217-9

RAFAELLO'S MISTRESS

First North American Publication 2001.

Visit us at www.eHarlequin.com

Printed in U.S.A.

CHAPTER ONE

WHEN Glory walked into the London headquarters of Grazzini Industries, every male head in the vicinity swivelled to watch her.

Her face was unforgettable: wide slanted cheekbones, bright eyes the colour of bluebells and a wide, full pink mouth. Even with her honey-blonde hair caught back, and clad in khaki combats and a casual top, she attracted attention. All the men stared: they couldn't help themselves. That stunning face and lush figure endowed her with an extraordinary degree of sex appeal.

Impervious to the attention that she was receiving, Glory was engaged in frantically talking up her flagging courage. Rafaello would listen to her, *of course* he would listen. So what if it had been five years since they had last met? So what if they had parted on bad terms? He had hurt her so much that even now she could not bring herself to recall how she had felt back then but she knew she had not hurt him. Powerful, influential businessmen were not known for their sensitivity. Maybe she had dented his ego a little but then he had never suffered from any lack in that department. She wouldn't be at all surprised to discover that Rafaello barely recalled their painfully brief fling.

Yet she remembered every day, every hour, every minute. She remembered how naïve and trusting and stupid she had been. She remembered that last night she had hoped to spend with him and the resulting humiliation followed by the agony of loss and rejection. The oldest story in the book, she told herself, fighting to suppress those debilitating memories. She had wanted love but he had only wanted a temporary distraction. He might so easily have become her first lover but they had broken up before she trusted him enough to say yes.

Left alone in the steel-walled lift as it climbed higher and higher, Glory rested her hot, damp brow against the cooling metal surface. Pull yourself together, girl. Chin up, hold your head high. Never mind that her nerves were eating her alive. Or that her wardrobe did not run to a smart suit. Or that she felt horribly intimidated by Rafaello's giant steel and glass office building. None of that mattered, she told herself. She was here to help her family: her dad, her kid brother, Sam.

Stepping out on to the top floor into an atmosphere of exclusive comfort and elegance, Glory approached the smart reception desk.

'I have an appointment with Mr Grazzini…' Her voice emerged all small and crushed by the sheer weight of her nervous tension.

The attractive brunette looked her up and down with a faint frownline etched between her perfect pencilled brows. 'Your name, Miss…?'

'Little. Glory Little,' Glory supplied hurriedly.

'Please take a seat…' The cool ice-blue leather seating area was indicated.

Glory reached for a glossy women's magazine. She flicked through fashion pages adorned by women wearing single garments that cost more than she earned in six months. Interest wandering, she glanced around herself, hugely impressed by her surroundings but anything but comfortable with them. Though it was certainly no surprise to her that Rafaello was doing extravagantly well in business. He had started out rich and would no doubt go on getting richer. Didn't it run in his genes? He had once told her that the Grazzini clan had started coining it as merchants during the Middle Ages.

No wonder they hadn't ended up together, she reflected, striving to see the humour of her own pitiful ignorance at the age of eighteen. Youthful bravado had persuaded her that things like different backgrounds and what some people called 'breeding' didn't matter in a world approaching the second millennium. To think otherwise was incredibly old-fashioned, she had told a less naïve friend, who had implied that Rafaello could only be after 'one thing'. When her father had tried to warn her off too, she had just laughed and pointed out that Rafaello didn't give two hoots about silly stuff, like her having left school at sixteen!

'Miss Little...?'

Snatched from her teeming thoughts, Glory glanced up to see a young man in a smart suit studying her. Clutching her bag, she got up. 'Yes?'

'Mr Grazzini will see you now.'

Glory managed a rather strained version of her usual sunny smile and looked down at her watch. 'Right on the dot of ten o'clock. Rafaello hasn't changed a bit. He was always dead keen on punctuality.'

In receipt of that chatty response, the young man looked taken aback. Glory flushed, hot embarrassed colour drenching her peaches and cream complexion right to the roots of her hair. She had said more than was required and city people didn't gush like that and offer up unnecessary facts at the drop of a hat. But nerves had always run away with Glory's tongue and, given the chance, she tended to rush to fill every awkward silence. Not this time, however. She knew why he had looked momentarily astonished and knowing did nothing for her self-esteem. The guy just could not imagine someone as ordinary as her *ever* having been on first-name terms with his rich and sophisticated employer.

'I'm Mr Grazzini's executive assistant,' he informed her. 'The name's Jon...Jon Lyons.'

'My name's Glory,' she said in turn, grateful her companion wasn't being as stand-offish as she had expected and scolding herself for her own prejudice.

'Very unusual…' Jon Lyons, who was traversing the wide corridor that lay before them at the crawling speed of a snail, paused to throw her a warm and appreciative smile. 'But very apt.'

Glory resisted the temptation to tell him that she owed her name to the fact that her father had celebrated his only daughter's birth rather too thoroughly and had then registered her name wrongly on her birth certificate. Instead of getting to be the lofty-sounding Gloriana as her fond mother had planned, she had ended up just being called Glory. Being only five feet one inch tall and blessed with a surname like Little, she was well-accustomed to being teased. And if Jon Lyons was trying to flirt with her, she didn't want to know.

At the age of twenty-three, she had met far too many men whose sole interest in her related to her embarrassingly lush curves. Dates that turned into wrestling sessions followed by aggrieved and aggressive 'Why nots?' had figured all too often in her experience. She cringed from that male attitude, found it demeaning and threatening. It was as if her body wasn't her own and she was expected to share it whether she wanted to or not. Being bone-deep stubborn and determined to hang on in there waiting for love and commitment, she had always been punitively mean in the sharing stakes.

Her companion kept on trying to chat her up but she played dumb. The closer they got to the imposing door and the foot of the corridor, the more enervated she became and her steps grew shorter and slower. Rafaello would be on the other side of that door waiting for her. But he had agreed to see her, hadn't he? Wasn't that hopeful? At least, his secretary had come back to her with an appointment fairly quickly and she wasn't fool enough to think that she could have got that far without Rafaello's agreement. Rafaello was rich and important and much in demand. She was really lucky that he was giving her the chance to speak up in her family's defence, she reminded herself.

So what was she actually going to say to Rafaello? Please, please think again? Please don't sack my father? Please don't blame him for my kid brother's antics?

Sam had done a stupid, stupid thing. Helping himself to the keys entrusted to their parent during the housekeeper's overnight absence, Sam had thrown an impromptu party in the Grazzini family's fabulous English home, Montague Park. The party had got out of hand. Panicking at the damage being done, Sam had run to their father for help. Then their father had made *his* mistake. Instead of admitting his son's guilt, her father had foolishly and unsuccessfully attempted to cover Sam's tracks and deny his involvement. Paling as she contemplated the challenge of trying to excuse such dishonest behaviour, Glory walked in through the door spread wide for her. Once over the threshold, she froze.

Her companion, who had remained in the corridor, had to nudge her a few inches deeper into the room to get the door closed behind her. Dry-mouthed, Glory scanned the vast office, her attention jumping from the contemporary glass and wrought-iron furniture to the wall of tinted glass windows and the sheer luxury of so much unoccupied and wholly unnecessary space. Where was Rafaello? Appreciating that he had yet to join her, she breathed in deeply and slowly exhaled again, fighting to get a firmer grip on herself.

But her own mind was working against her like a secret enemy. As she stood there doing the careful breathing exercises that a magazine article had said were a great aid to achieving a calm state of mind, she started getting something rather akin to flashbacks. Her first true sighting of Rafaello Grazzini eight years earlier...

Glory's father, Archie Little, was the head gardener at Montague Park. Just as his father had been and his father before him, for her ancestors had worked on the Montague estate for a couple of centuries. About seventy-odd years back, Rafaello's grandfather had married the last of the Montague line and had resisted all pleas to assume his wife's maiden name. The fair and rather chinless Montagues had been replaced by the infinitely more exotic and good-looking Grazzinis with their dark flashing eyes and aggressive jawlines.

Before her father became head gardener the Littles had lived in the village several miles from Montague Park, but when he was promoted he had been provided with a comfortable cottage on the estate. Her parents had been delighted but Glory had been distraught because all her friends had lived in the village. Being stuck in the midst of several thousand acres of beautiful unspoilt countryside had seemed to her a fate worse than death.

One afternoon soon after that move, out walking and still wallowing in self-pity, Glory had enjoyed one of those rare life-changing experiences: she had seen Rafaello Grazzini on a scrambler motorbike, racing a friend with a breathtaking lack of caution for his own safety. No youthful male had ever appeared to greater advantage to an impressionable fifteen-year-old girl than he did that day. She had watched him wheeling the powerful bike to a halt and wrenching off his helmet. His black hair had blown back from his vibrant dark features, strong and bold against the washed-out colours of a too dry English summer. Glory had discovered right there and then that living in the rural depths had one major consolation: Rafaello Grazzini, six years older, and unlikely to notice she occupied the same earth but very worthy of becoming the target of her first besotted crush.

Only somewhere along the line something had gone wrong, Glory conceded dully. She had *not* outgrown the crush. Even when he had maddened and mortified her beyond belief in an unfortunate first encounter the following year, she had stayed dangerously loyal and keen. And when, two years later, all her dreams came true and she actually went *out* with Rafaello it had taken precious little encouragement for her to move from the base of that juvenile infatuation into being passionately in love.

Without warning, a door on the far side of the office opened. Sprung from her unwelcome mental trawl back through past events, Glory jumped as though someone had fired a gun behind her and spun round.

'I'm afraid I was waylaid by one of the directors,' Rafaello murmured, cool as a long drink of icy water on a hot day.

Glory was trembling and she couldn't help herself. It had been five years since she had seen him. Five long years that had taken her from girl to woman but, in the blink of an eye, all that painfully acquired maturity was wrenched from her by the simple act of Rafaello walking into the same room. She gazed at him in shock, for nothing could have prepared her for the strength of her own reaction. At eighteen, her cure had been steadily and repeatedly telling herself that she had romanticised and embellished her image of him beyond belief. And there he stood, every inch of him a blatant rejection of such wishful thinking...

Six feet two inches tall, much taller than she had allowed him to be in her memory, and with the wide shoulders, broad chest, narrow hips and long muscular legs of a natural athlete. Not even that formal fine grey pinstripe suit so superbly tailored to his powerful frame could shield her from the acknowledgement that whatever he had been doing in recent years he had not been allowing himself to run to seed.

Having only reached as high in her appraisal as the pristine white collar encircling the elegant knot on his dark red silk tie, Glory tipped her head back and ran headlong into the stunning effect of brilliant dark eyes fringed by inky individual lashes that stood out against his smooth olive skin. Mouth dry and heart suddenly racing so fast that it felt as if it was lodged in her throat, Glory just stared back, dragged at terrifying speed up onto the heights of helpless excitement.

'Take a seat,' Rafaello urged with complete calm.

Her big blue eyes widened slightly. All around her the atmosphere was churning with so much fiery tension that she felt dizzy. Yet he was not turning a single strand of that luxuriant black hair so well-styled to his arrogant dark head. He felt nothing...he felt *nothing*, Glory realised, and she felt gutted. Even as he went through the polite motions of lifting a chair with one lean brown hand and planting it helpfully beside her, she was incapable of suppressing the sudden violent rise of tempestuous emotion attacking her.

Memory and bitter pain seemed to coalesce inside her. She saw the worst moment of her life afresh. Five years ago. Rafaello kissing that snobby redhead whose father was a merchant banker, standing Glory up in the restaurant that had been *their* place. His well-bred friends had been very amused by her tearful flight but equally relieved that Rafaello had dumped the gardener's daughter with her local-yokel accent and lack of further education.

Stepping behind her, Rafaello curved light hands to her stiff arms and guided her down into the chair. Like a child who had just seen a very nasty accident, she sat there staring straight ahead of her while she crushed out that tormenting recollection of her humiliation and sought to resurrect her defences.

'When people ask to see me, they usually talk a mile a minute because my time is valuable,' Rafaello spelt out in the same collected dark drawl.

'Maybe I don't know what to say...I mean, it's kind of traumatic...I mean, *awkward*,' Glory stressed in an uneven rush, 'seeing you again...'

Rafaello strolled with fluid grace back into her line of vision. He lounged back against the edge of his fancy desk and dealt her a smooth smile that somehow turned her churning tummy cold as ice. 'I don't feel at all awkward, Glory.'

Glory focused on his tie with deadly concentration. 'Well, I'm sure you're not wondering what I'm doing here, so I'll just get on with it…'

'Hopefully,' Rafaello encouraged.

Just when she was about to break into her prepared speech, her mind went blank again on the helpless acknowledgement that she just loved his voice: that husky Italian accent that purred along every syllable and transformed the plainest word into something special. Something special that danced down her spine like a caress. *Caress?*

Cheeks crimsoning, Glory broke back into harried speech. 'First I want to say how very sorry I am for what my brother did. Sam was very much in the wrong. I mean, he was brought up to respect other people's property just as I was but he's very young—'

'I am aware of that,' Rafaello said rather drily. 'Do you think you could bring yourself to look me in the face? It's rather distracting to have someone addressing my tie.'

A nervous giggle bubbled up in Glory's throat and escaped in a rather choky sound. She lifted her chin, tilted back her honey-blonde head.

'Better, *cara*,' Rafaello pronounced, gazing at her with hooded dark eyes that gave her the shivers all over again.

'It's not really better for me,' Glory muttered helplessly. 'I'm so nervous that I keep on forgetting what I'm saying.'

'Nervous? Of me?' Rafaello purred like a prowling predator. 'Surely not?'

All of a sudden, she felt controlled. Like a little toy train being wound up and set on a circular track he had already laid out. She stared at him. Lethal, dark and dangerous but so undeniably gorgeous that the average woman forgot the danger. He was so still, almost as if he was letting her gaze her fill, and suddenly she was past caring and greedy where minutes earlier she had been cautious. That lean bronzed face had haunted her dreams but had always blurred in daylight. The hard, high cheekbones, the strong nose, the beautiful, sensual mouth. She was looking for the cruelty that she had found in him too late to protect herself. But all she could recognise was his aura of tempered steel toughness, his incredibly intimidating self-command and the amount of authority he could put out even when in a relaxed pose.

'Let's chat for a while,' Rafaello suggested, stretching out a lean hand to stab a button on some piece of office equipment and ordering coffee for two. 'I doubt that we have any herbal tea on the premises.'

'Coffee will be fine.' *Chat?* Chat about what? What did they have to chat about?

'Where are you living now?' Rafaello enquired casually.

'Near where I work—'

'With?'

'Nobody. It's a bedsit—'

'In?'

'A house…?' Glory asked, transfixed by the questions flying like bullets at her and unable to keep up.

Rafaello sighed. 'I meant…where is the bedsit situated?'

'Birmingham,' she told him.

'I always thought of you as a country girl.'

'There aren't many jobs going in the country these days,' Glory pointed out tightly, thinking that his idea of chatting more closely resembled an interrogation. But then why shouldn't he be curious? Being curious was only human, wasn't it?

'So where do you work?'

The knock on the door and the rattle of approaching china came as a welcome interruption. Obviously coffee was always on offer at the speed of light: a tray sitting already prepared and some fancy machine ready to dispense the hot, viciously strong brew he favoured. Her mind was going all over the place again. He never had taken to her herbal tea, Glory recalled dimly.

'You were saying…?' As a china cup and saucer were slid onto the small table that had appeared by her elbow by someone she did not even have the time to look at, Rafaello returned to his rather forbidding concept of casual chat.

'Was I?' Glory reached for the coffee. 'Oh, yes, where I work. A factory—'

'What kind of factory?'

'Well…it's nothing very interesting…'

Brilliant dark eyes settled on her. 'You might be surprised at what interests me.'

Glory jerked a slight shoulder in submission and her coffee slopped out of the cup into the saucer. 'The factory makes polystyrene for packaging and all sorts of other things…'

Rafaello continued to observe her as though her every word was fascinating. 'And what do you do there?'

'I pack it…the polystyrene. Sometimes I do other jobs—'

Rafaello was studying her with intense concentration. 'And for how long have you been thrilling to the excitement of the factory floor?'

'Look, it's not exciting but I work alongside a nice bunch of people and the pay's not bad.' Her beautiful eyes reflecting reproach at that tone of sarcasm, Glory coloured. 'I've been there two years.'

'Forgive me for asking, *cara*,' Rafaello drawled softly, 'but what happened to your burning ambition to become a model?'

Glory paled and stiffened. 'It wasn't exactly a burning ambition. As you know, I had that offer and it…well, it just didn't pan out—'

'Why not?'

The pink tip of her tongue snaked out to moisten the taut

line of her lower lip. She was extremely uncomfortable with his line of questioning and dismayed by the extent of his interest. His dark gaze dropped to her soft, full mouth and lingered with visible force. Sudden tension seemed to make the atmosphere sizzle. She felt her lips tingle as if he were touching them and her breathing seemed to choke off at source. Her bra felt too tight for her full breasts and her nipples pinched tight into straining buds of sensitivity. In dismay, she began sipping at the coffee she didn't want with a hand that shook. Please no, she was praying, please, no, don't let me be feeling like this again...

'Why not?' Rafaello persisted without remorse. 'Why didn't the modelling offer work out?'

He was going to dig and dig until he hit paydirt, Glory registered in mortification, and so she decided to just be honest. 'It wasn't the kind of modelling I wouldn've done. It was what they call "glamour" stuff...you know...like where you take your clothes off for the camera, rather than put clothes on?'

Rafaello surveyed her steadily, not a muscle moving on his darkly handsome face.

'So they asked you to get your kit off...and you said no? Didn't they offer you enough money?'

Glory looked at him in considerable embarrassment. 'The money had nothing to do with it. I just wasn't prepared to *do* that sort of stuff—'

Rafaello dealt her a look of derision. 'I didn't come down in the last shower of rain, *cara*. Are you or are you not the woman my father bought off with five thousand pounds?'

At that unexpected question, Glory turned whiter than his shirt and stared back at him in horror. As her fingers involuntarily loosened their grip on the saucer it fell clean out of her hand. The cup tipped and she gasped as coffee went flying over the perfect pale carpet.

'*Si*...yes,' Rafaello confirmed as the spilt liquid flowed over the expensive fibres in a spreading stain and she just stared fixedly at it, paralysed where she sat. 'Naturally my father told me what it cost to persuade you that I was not, after all, the love of your life. And it was a fitting footnote to our relationship. A lousy five grand when you could have had ten, twenty, thirty times that for the asking. But I guess five grand seemed like a small fortune to you then.'

Glory was still watching the seeping pool of coffee. She was appalled that he had found out about that payment. She felt sick. She was in an agony of shame. Rafaello knew, Rafaello *knew* about the money. 'He said it would be a secret, he said you would never know…' she mumbled strickenly.

'*Dio mio*…do you believe everything you're told?' Rafaello murmured with a cruel enjoyment that she could feel like a knife plunging between her ribs. 'I was amused—'

'Amused?' Folding her arms over her churning tummy, Glory gazed up at him in shaken disbelief.

'My father acting like some clumsy Victorian squire trying to pay off a maidservant he saw as a threat to family unity. So unnecessary,' Rafaello mused. 'I never entertained a single serious thought about our relationship. But I *wasn't* amused when you took the money like the greedy little gold-digger he said you were. That was cheap and inexcusable.'

Glory sat there as if she were turned to stone. She said nothing. She had nothing to say, for, as the money had not been returned, she could not defend herself. It would scarcely help her father's case if she was now to confide that Archie Little had refused to allow her to destroy that cheque. Indeed, he had taken her to the bank that same day and the money had been transferred into his account. Beggars couldn't be choosers, he had said when she argued with him. If she was being forced to leave home to please Benito Grazzini, her father had believed that he was due some compensation. Deprived of her help in the household, not to mention the extra money her job brought in, how was he to manage?

A greedy little gold-digger? So that was how Rafaello had learned to think of her over the past five years. True bitterness scythed through Glory. She thought of the games rich people played and the damage they could wreak. Their money could give them the power to bully smaller people and make them do what they didn't want to do. She had left home because her father's job and his very survival had been at stake and for no other reason. It seemed bitterly ironic that she was now facing Rafaello again for much the same reason.

She squared her shoulders and veiled her eyes. 'Now that you've told me what you think of me, can we discuss why I asked for this appointment?'

'Go ahead...' Rafaello said drily.

'You've given my father a month's notice—'

'Don't tell me you're surprised.' Rafaello elevated a sleek dark brow. 'If it hadn't been for your father's incompetence, your punk of a brother would never have gained access to my home—'

'Sam nicked the keys when Dad was asleep,' Glory protested, rising to her feet in a sudden defensive movement. 'Since Dad could hardly have guessed what Sam was planning to do, you can't blame him for what happened!'

'But I can certainly blame your father for telling the police a pack of lies and trying to protect your brother and his nasty destructive friends,' Rafaello cut in with ruthless bite. 'Have you any idea how much damage has been caused to the Park?'

'Sam told me everything.' However, Glory's combative stance had instantly evaporated when she was faced with that daunting question. 'Rugs stained and furniture scratched and windows broken, but at least the damage was restricted to two rooms. As soon as Sam realised that his mates were too drunk for him to control, he ran for help.

Dad should have called the police himself and he should have told the truth when the housekeeper called the police in the next morning—'

'But he *didn't*,' Rafaello slotted in with lethal timing.

'He was scared of the consequences. My brother's only sixteen. But Sam *did* tell the truth when the police questioned him. He's very ashamed and very sorry—'

'Of course he is. He doesn't want to be prosecuted.'

Having turned noticeably paler at that blunt statement of possible intent, Glory said in desperation, 'Didn't you ever kick up a lark that went horribly wrong at his age?'

'If you're asking, did I ever trespass on someone else's property or vandalise it?...the answer is *no*.'

'But then, I bet you had more exciting outlets at Sam's age,' Glory persisted. 'Only there's virtually nothing for teenagers to do in the area and nowhere for them to go either. None of them have any money—'

'Cut the bleeding-heart routine,' Rafaello advised with cold impatience. 'I've got no time for anyone who violates either my home or my property. The clean-up bill alone will run into thousands—'

'*Thousands?*' she stressed in astonishment.

She received a nod of confirmation.

'You're being ripped off!' Glory told him. 'Everybody knows that you're loaded. I bet you're being quoted a crazy figure for the clean-up because the firm knows you can afford it.'

Rafaello surveyed her with sardonic cool. 'Glory...it takes highly trained professionals to repair valuable antiques and restore damaged plasterwork. That kind of expertise comes at a premium charge.'

Feeling very foolish, feeling all the confused embarrassment of someone who had not a clue about the care of antiques, Glory subsided and set off doggedly on another tack. 'I feel awful that we can't offer you any financial compensation—'

'I feel awful that sentencing tearaway teenagers to thirty lashes has gone out of fashion,' Rafaello imparted very drily. 'But the return of the snuff box that was removed from the drawing-room might…just *might* persuade me not to prosecute your brother.'

Glory had gone very still. 'Something was—er—taken? But why didn't the police mention that to Sam yesterday?'

'They weren't aware of it until this morning when *I* realised that it was missing,' Rafaello explained grimly. 'The snuff box is tiny and would've been easily slipped into a pocket.'

'A snuff box?' Glory parrotted weakly, aghast at the news that an item of value might have been stolen from the Park, for that was an infinitely more serious offence.

'German, eighteenth century, made of gold and covered with precious stones. It will be virtually impossible to replace,' Rafaello outlined.

Glory parted her taut lips. 'How much is it worth?'

'About sixty grand.'

Glory tried and failed to swallow. 'Sixty thousand… *pounds*?'

'I have excellent taste—'

'And you think it's been stolen?' Glory exclaimed. 'I mean, have you searched? Are you *sure*?'

'I would not have reported it to the police otherwise. It puts rather a different complexion on your touching portrayal of bored teenagers with nowhere to go and nothing to do, and I have every intention of pressing charges on the score of that theft.'

Her lips bloodlessly compressed and her knees wobbling, Glory sank down almost clumsily into the seat she had vacated mere minutes before. 'No way would Sam have stolen anything—'

'Someone did.'

Her head felt as if it was going round and round. The situation was even worse than she had realised. There had been around twenty teenagers at that impromptu party. Any one of them could have lifted something small without attracting attention. A tiny box worth *sixty* thousand pounds? She felt physically sick. Sam having let himself into the huge house to throw a party for his drunken friends had been serious enough…but theft as well?

'Obviously you're planning to press charges against Sam and you have no intention of changing your mind about dismissing my dad.' Glory could see that she had no hope of dissuading him on either count now.

'Did you think I would be so overwhelmed by your fabulous face and body that I would write it all off for old times' sake?' Rafaello murmured softly and smoothly but she felt his contempt right down into her bones and recoiled from it.

'No…but I had to *try* to reason with you,' she stressed shakily, looking up to encounter hard dark eyes with a shocking sense of betrayal. She could neither bear nor yet accept how low she had sunk in his estimation. 'My father and my brother deserve to be in trouble for being stupid but you're talking about wrecking their lives. Dad's got no fancy gardening qualifications and he won't get another job at his age. All because of this snuff box going missing? What do you need with a stupid box costing that much anyway?'

'Beautiful things give me pleasure,' Rafaello admitted without hesitation.

'Is there anything I can say or do…?' Glory demanded feverishly.

'You're asking *me* to advise you on how to change *my* mind?' Rafaello slung her a sardonic appraisal and then he vented a husky laugh. 'What have you got to offer me in return?'

'Undying gratitude?' Glory suggested without much hope.

'Something for nothing is not my style. Perhaps you

should appeal to my baser instincts. Let me think. What do *I* want that *you* can give me?' Rafaello rested dark deep-set eyes that were shimmering with glints of awakening on her taut seated figure. 'Only one thing. Sex.'

CHAPTER TWO

SEX? What sort of a crack was that to make? Glory released a nervous laugh. Eyes very wide and blue pinned to him, she muttered unevenly, 'You don't mean that...you don't mean that like it sounds.'

'Don't I? I'm the guy you sold out for a derogatory five grand. You'll never convince me that moral standards are a subject likely to keep you awake at night,' Rafaello murmured in a hypnotically quiet undertone that rasped down her taut spine like sandpaper on silk. 'So what about it, Glory?'

'What about *what*?' Glory snapped half an octave higher, still refusing to credit that he could actually mean what he was saying and springing restively upright again. She pushed back a straying strand of honey-blonde hair from her brow in a defensive movement. 'Is this your idea of a joke?'

'A joke? Far from it. You should be flattered.' Lounging at his ease, Rafaello gazed steadily back at her. 'I'm offering to whisk you off the factory floor and install you in my bed while at the same time allowing your useless male relatives off the hook. Now if that's not generous, what is?'

'You're just saying this stuff to humiliate me because you don't like me—'

'Glory...I don't need to like or respect you to want you under me, over me and any other way I can think of having you,' Rafaello countered with level cool, his unapologetic bluntness in delineating that earthy reality shattering what few illusions she still retained.

'How can you talk to me like this?' Glory demanded half

under her breath, her damp hands clenching into fists by her sides.

'Don't knock the lust factor when it can work to your advantage. Even dressed as you are now, you're gorgeous.' Rafaello ran brilliant dark golden eyes over the full swell of her breasts below the sweater, let his meaningful scrutiny of her charms slide to the pronounced curve of her hips below her tiny waist and then lower still.

She stood there with her face burning. She felt that unashamedly male appraisal like a flame of sexual contempt singeing her sensitive skin. But, worst of all, she was experiencing sensations she had almost forgotten she *could* feel. That enervating little tightening *frisson* of physical response low in her pelvis, the mortifying sensation of liquid heat between her clenching thighs.

'I don't want to hear any more!' she gasped, spinning away from him, sucking in a stark breath, fighting to stop her body reacting to the erotic buzz in the atmosphere, to *him*.

'But the more I contemplate the possibilities, the more I warm up to the idea, *cara*,' Rafaello confided huskily. 'Straightforward sex. An honest agreement, free of all those restrictive relationship complexities. I keep you…and you please me.'

'You are not going to keep me and I am *not* going to bed with you, Rafaello Grazzini!' Glory launched at him furiously. 'I'm not a whore!'

'You have…' with offensive detachment, Rafaello shrugged back his shirt cuff to glance at the narrow gold watch on his strong wrist '…three and a half hours to make your mind up. If you're not back here by two this afternoon, the offer is closed.'

Aghast at that level announcement, Glory stared at him with shaken bright blue eyes, finally accepting that he was serious. 'Do you honestly think that I would trade my body—?'

'To the highest bidder? *Yes*,' Rafaello incised without hesitation. 'Five years ago, I was very slow to catch on to what you really wanted from me. I didn't give you any expensive gifts. Nor did it occur to me to put cold, hard cash on the table and pay the price for the intimacy I wanted—'

'Stop it!' Glory exclaimed in angry chagrined despair, whirling away from him again to conceal her pained mortification. 'It wasn't like that between us.'

'You took money to stay out of my bed. Presumably you would've accepted a better offer to get into it!'

'No, I wouldn't have done!' Inflamed by that assertion, Glory turned back to yell at him, her voice breaking with distress, 'I *loved* you!'

'Only you couldn't love me to the value of five grand?' Rafaello shot her a derisive appraisal and then his expressive mouth curled into a hard smile of chilling amusement. 'You've got some nerve telling me that.'

'I hate you...' Glory bit out with a shudder of violent resentment at the humiliation he was inflicting on her. 'I really hate you now.'

'I can live with that...I can live with that fine.' Arrogant dark head high, brilliant eyes level, Rafaello surveyed her as if she had thrown down a gauntlet and challenged him.

'You won't be *asked* to live with it!' Glory shot at him tempestuously, stalking back to the chair to snatch up her bag. Her beautiful face was furiously flushed, her blue eyes bright as sapphires with anger. 'Does it give you a cheap thrill to think that you have power over me?'

'I don't call writing off a debt of eighty grand cheap. As to the power—how do I feel about that? Pretty damned good, *cara*,' Rafaello confided.

'You don't have power over me. You have no power unless I *give* it to you!' Glory snapped back in so much rage she could hardly vocalise.

'But you'd do anything for your father and your brother.

Do you think I don't know that? Where are the spineless cowards lurking, anyway?'

'What are you talking about?'

'Archie and Sam. I notice they're conspicuous by their absence,' Rafaello extended with perceptible scorn as he strolled to the door with fluid grace and held it open for her, demonstrating an inbred courtesy that set her teeth on edge even more. 'But then, maybe it was your idea to come alone in their place—'

At that moment, Glory was past caring what he thought of her, for she only wanted to escape. 'Maybe it was—'

'Maybe you fancied your chances with me again—'

'You really think you're something, don't you?' she condemned between compressed lips.

'At the very least, cleverer than you are. Either you should have brought the male back-up or sat weeping and whingeing until revulsion wore me down—'

'I don't weep or whinge!'

'I wouldn't want you if you did.' Rafaello focused on Jon Lyons, who was standing down at the reception area at the far end of the corridor, trying not to look as if he was watching them. He skimmed his attention back to her with derisive dark eyes that sent a wave of colour flaming across her slanted cheekbones. 'Five minutes here and you've got my executive assistant panting at your heels like a pet dog. Do him a favour. Give him the big freeze on the way out!'

'Go to hell!' she hissed and stalked away, shivering with rage and shame and bitterness.

For what could she do and what could she possibly say to defend herself? Rafaello thought she was greedy and unscrupulous. Whether she liked it or not, she had to accept that five years ago she had made a serious error of judgement and now she was paying the price for it. She had allowed her father to take that cheque for five thousand pounds and *keep* it. Archie Little had been in debt and desperate for money. After Glory had endured that demeaning interview with Rafaello's father she hadn't had enough fight left in her to resist her own parent's demands and stand up for what was right. She had felt microscopic in size by the time Benito Grazzini had finished talking to her. He had left her with few illusions about the myth of social equality.

Yet she had still sensed that Rafaello's father did not like what he was doing any more than she had liked having such cruel pressure put on her. He had just wanted her out of his son's life and had evidently decided that the end must justify the means. So he had pointed out that he would be well within his rights if he dismissed her father for his less than adequate job performance at that time. She had known that, shorn of stability of both home and employment, her father would have never found the strength to get his life back on track.

In that same year, six months before Glory reached her eighteenth birthday and before she even went out with Rafaello, her stable, happy home life had begun to unravel at the seams. Without the smallest warning her mother, Talitha, had died—a heart attack—there one moment, gone the next. Her mother had been the strong one in her parents' marriage and the cement that held their family together. Her father had gone to pieces and hit the bottle hard.

Glory had found herself engaged in a constant losing battle to keep the older man sober. No matter how hard she struggled to support him, he had often been in no state to work and on many occasions he had simply wandered off during working hours to drink himself into a stupor. Most employers would have sacked him. But, surprisingly, Benito Grazzini had been sympathetic towards the grieving widower and he had kept on giving Archie Little another chance to straighten himself out. That reality had given him strong ammunition when he asked Glory to leave her home.

'Look at your family background and tell me that you

are not wrong for my son. I believe that it is best for everyone concerned that *you* should move away and make a fresh start somewhere else,' Rafaello's father had pronounced with the harshness of a man who had steeled himself to perform an unpleasant duty. 'In return I will promise to do all that is within my power to help your father overcome his problems.'

Her *background*. No further explanation had been required once that word had been spoken. Her once respected father had been behaving like a drunken layabout, and her late mother? Talitha Little had never won local acceptance, for she had been born and bred a gypsy. In Romany parlance, she had 'married out' and once she had made that choice custom had demanded that even her own family have nothing more to do with her. Yet the new life she had chosen with her *gadjo* husband, Archie Little, had been no more welcoming. Her herbal lore and superstitious ways had been foreign and threatening to her village neighbours. Talitha had much preferred the privacy of their isolated woodland cottage on the Montague estate.

As Glory re-entered the lift on the top floor of Grazzini Industries she was too worked up even to register Jon Lyons' hovering presence nearby. Her brother and her father were waiting for her in a café near the train station. She wondered what on earth she was going to tell them. That Rafaello Grazzini had made her an offer she could not accept? That she would sooner boil in oil than be any man's kept woman? But most especially *his*?

Oh, yes, most especially *his* woman! Distraught with the strength of the conflicting feelings attacking her, Glory hurried through the crowded city streets. Why was Rafaello doing this to her? Five years ago, they had only been together six weeks. Long enough for her to fall irrevocably in love but not long enough to persuade her to surrender her virginity to a male who had made not the smallest mention of love.

She could thank her mother for that ingrained caution. Talitha Little had believed that a woman's most precious possession was purity, for that was exactly how she had been raised. When Glory had first been given that message she had not even properly understood what physical intimacy was. But long before she reached the age of temptation she had absorbed the unnerving impression that her life would go horribly wrong if she broke that rule before she was safely married.

Rafaello had thought that was hilariously funny until he realised over the space of several weeks that Glory was serious. Then he had suggested it was a little weird and that, with all due respect to her late mother's convictions, Glory really should not let herself be affected by such superstitious fears.

Emerging from that recollection, Glory discovered that she was lodged stock-still in front of a shop window and smiling with a silly far-away look fixed to her face. Her smile died. As she crushed out that ruefully amusing recollection of Rafaello's efforts to persuade her into his bed, her dulled eyes stung with hot tears of regret.

She walked on, striving to concentrate and find a solution to her family's predicament. Sam was a minor in the eyes of the law and Rafaello could press charges to his heart's content, but he had no proof whatsoever that her kid brother had been involved in the theft of that snuff box. The worst that was likely to happen to Sam was…what? A police caution? Sam had never been in trouble before and how would he bear up to that challenge?

'Sam's different,' Glory's mother had once muttered in exasperation. 'He's too sensitive and emotional for a boy. He'll get the life teased out of him if he doesn't toughen up.' Happily, Sam's talent on the sports field had made him popular at school. But he had once shaken Glory with the admission that he hated sport of all kinds. She wondered how many of his friends knew that Sam spent every spare moment sketching people and animals. Or that sometimes Sam listened to depressing items on the news and became deeply upset by them, that he took things too much to heart.

And what about her father? Might he fall off the wagon and begin drinking again? He was a kind man, a good man, but he was weak, she acknowledged painfully. In times of trouble, he crumpled.

Her father and her brother were seated at the back of the half-empty café nursing cups of tea. Their eyes flew to her as she drew level with their table. She sat down beside her brother, deeply troubled by the misery that he could not hide.

'What did Mr Grazzini say?' her father demanded, his lined brow furrowed beneath his greying blond hair, his faded blue eyes red-rimmed with the effects of strain and insufficient sleep. He looked older than his fifty-seven years and drained.

'Dad…'

'It's bad, isn't it? If only this had happened before Benito Grazzini retired and handed over the estate to his son,' Archie Little muttered in a bitter tone of defeat. 'That Rafaello's as hard as nails. I don't know what you ever saw in him, Glory. But nothing I could say would turn you away from him—'

'Sam,' Glory cut in hurriedly, turning to address her brother before her father could say anything more in a similar vein. There was little resemblance between brother and sister, because Sam was much taller with very dark hair and dark eyes. He had taken after their mother's side of the family, while she had inherited their father's fair colouring. But right now, for all his size and athletic breadth, Sam looked very much like a scared ten-year-old kid.

'What happened?' her brother prompted anxiously.

'Rafaello told me that a very valuable snuff box went missing while you and your friends were partying—'

'Are you saying something was stolen? Well, it couldn't

have been any of us!' Sam gave his sister a shocked look of reproach. 'Do you think we're stupid?'

'You need to pass the word round your friends that that box must be returned, because Rafaello is not going to let it go. It's worth a great deal of money.'

'I didn't see *any* of my mates with a box,' Sam told her with a perplexed frown.

'Rafaello said it was tiny…small enough to be hidden in a pocket,' Glory informed him, and she was relieved at the need to make that explanation to her brother, for his ignorance satisfied her that he could have had nothing to do with the theft.

Listening to that dialogue between his son and daughter, Archie Little had turned a sickly grey shade. 'Something being stolen finishes us. No wonder you couldn't get anywhere with Rafaello Grazzini,' he said heavily. 'He'll be furious. Can't blame him either. Sam had enough cheek even going into the Park, never mind the damage he and his mates caused, and now *this*…'

'I'm sorry, Dad…' Sam mumbled chokily. 'I swear I'll never do anything like that again—'

'You're not likely to get the chance, son.' Rising wearily to his feet, the older man studied his troubled daughter and sighed. 'We'll go home now and you go on back to Birmingham. I'm sorry, Glory. I wish I hadn't dragged you into this mess.'

'Why did you think Rafaello would listen to me?' Glory could not help asking.

Her father sighed. 'Something your mother once said. You know, one of those strange notions she used to take…'

'What did she say?'

'That he would always look after you. Silly,' he said wryly. 'It didn't make sense then and it makes even less now.'

But those words that she had never heard before sent the oddest shiver down Glory's spine. Just before they parted outside the café, her brother grabbed her in a sudden bone-crushing hug that let her know just how frantic with worry he was. With tears in her eyes, she watched her brother and father walk away. She hadn't even been asked what had passed between her and Rafaello. But then, would she have told the truth *had* she been asked? The minute she had mentioned that stolen snuff box, her father had given up all hope of matters being settled more amicably.

And how did she feel now? Horribly guilty, she discovered, for protecting herself when she might have helped her father and brother. But at what cost might she have helped? By putting herself in the power of a male who despised her? Two wrongs did not make a right, and Rafaello had wronged her in his big flashy office. She should have told him that too, should have told him that he had had no business treating her like that. And while she was doing that she ought to have told him the unlovely truth about his *own* father's treatment of her five years earlier! Benito Grazzini might've informed Rafaello that she had taken that cheque for five thousand pounds. But she was darned sure that Rafaello's father had not also admitted the cruel pressure he had brought to bear on a frightened eighteen-year-old girl, fearful of the consequences to her family if she dared to stand up for herself!

In a sudden decisive movement, Glory turned in her tracks and headed back in the direction of Grazzini Industries. She was going to tell Rafaello Grazzini what she thought of him! And his lousy, rich, bullying father, that fine upstanding man whom Rafaello had always regarded with such immense respect. She wasn't the *only* one with embarrassing and dishonest relatives and it was time he faced that fact!

By the time Glory arrived on the top floor of Grazzini Industries for the second time that day, she was dizzy with the number of emotions buzzing about inside her. The receptionist called Rafaello on the phone.

'You can go straight in,' Glory was told.

What was she going to say to Rafaello? Was she really about to tell Rafaello that his father had broken her heart and that it had taken the meanest and nastiest blackmail to frighten her into giving him up? Did she really *want* to tell Rafaello that? Did his ego deserve the news that she had truly loved him to distraction five years ago? Indeed, exactly *why* was she back in his office building desperate to confront him again?

Suffering a sudden loss of confidence at the way her own mind worked, Glory hovered outside Rafaello's office door. An awful suspicion was growing on her by the minute. She could not entirely ignore the amount of exhilaration that the prospect of seeing him again induced inside her...

Disorientatingly while she was still engaged in her inner battle the door opened. '*Still* having second thoughts?' Rafaello murmured with expressionless cool.

Glory studied him. Her tongue was glued to the dry roof of her mouth. Her heart was suddenly beating so fast that she could hardly get breath into her straining lungs. That lean, strong face and those dark deep-set eyes of his. Having once made that visual connection, she could not break it. It was as if a very powerful magnet had been turned on her and she was too weak to fight the strength of that pull.

She gulped. 'Don't get this wrong. I came here...I came back here *solely* to give you a piece of my mind.'

'You can do it over lunch,' Rafaello countered in his lazy accented drawl, curving a casual arm around her spine to flip her round and urge her back in the direction of the lift again.

'Lunch?' Glory exclaimed, taken aback.

'I'm hungry.' Rafaello rested shimmering dark golden eyes on her. 'I am *so* hungry.'

Glory trembled, her bemused blue eyes sinking to the level of the sensual slant of his beautiful mouth and noting

the faint blue-tinged roughness of the skin on his strong
jawline. She recalled that he had always had to shave twice
a day. And that stray abstracted reflection somehow sent
her off on the memory of how he kissed, how he had once
made her feel. She had never truly appreciated the depth
of her own hunger for him until she had discovered that *no*
other man had the ability to send her temperature rocketing
as he had.

'Intense, isn't it, *cara*?' Rafaello purred like a big jungle
cat, emanating an amount of masculine satisfaction that
suddenly made her want to slap him hard and snapped her
free of the potent spell he cast for long enough to make
her think again.

Why had she come back? Had it been a case of grabbing
at any excuse just to see him again? For what good reason
had she raced back to Grazzini Industries? What had happened five years ago didn't matter any more. What he
thought of her no longer mattered either. And if her reap-
pearance had now given him entirely the wrong impression,
wasn't that her fault too?

'I've decided I don't want to give you a piece of my
mind any more,' Glory confided in a rush as he swept her
inexorably into the lift with him. 'I shouldn't *be* here, but
while I am here I might as well tell you that I told Sam
about that box and I'm absolutely convinced that he had
nothing to do with its disappearance—'

As Glory paused for the breath with which to continue,
Rafaello backed her into the corner of the lift and rested
his lean hands on her slight, tense shoulders. 'You're talking too much.'

'But Sam's going to pass the word round his friends, so
hopefully something will come from that, and I'm going
back to Birmingham,' Glory continued at an even faster
and more breathless trot. She was hugely aware of the lean,
powerful length of him within inches of her own taut body

and the wave of heat darting up through her no matter how hard she fought to hold it down.

'You're *not* going back to Birmingham...' Rafaello intoned, allowing his lean fingers to glide down her slender arms and then enclosing her smaller hands in his without warning.

'No!' Glory cried, yanking herself free of that imprisoning hold with the abruptness of a woman suddenly waking up to the threat. 'You're not listening to me, are you? I'm not accepting your offer. I want nothing to do with you—'

With a roughened groan of raw impatience, Rafaello meshed one hand into the soft coils of her honey-blonde hair to hold her still and he brought his mouth crashing down with hungry intensity on hers. For a split-second, she went rigid with shock and he took advantage. He backed her up against the cool metallic wall and splayed his hands beneath her hips to lift her up to him. And then he let his tongue drive between her parted lips with erotic force, plundering the tender interior within, and every nerve-ending in her quivering body went haywire.

She wrapped her arms round his neck and clung, kissing him back with mindless fervour. A tormented moan of response was dragged from low in her throat. She couldn't get enough of that drugging passion which she had once worked so hard to forget. The very strength and power of the hard male physique keeping her pinned back to the wall inflamed her with dangerous heat. Helpless in the grip of her own increasing excitement, she was beyond thought or objection when he splayed her thighs round him, the better to anchor her to him.

And then, without any warning whatsoever, Rafaello froze. With a ragged groan, he released her swollen mouth and gazed down at her with heavily lidded smouldering golden eyes that had a faintly dazed light. '*Per meraviglia...* We are in a lift in a public building!'

In an equally sudden movement, Rafaello settled her back down onto her own feet. In shock, Glory finally realised that the lift was still and that all the lights on the control panel were flashing but that the doors had yet to open. 'Why isn't it moving?'

'I stopped it,' Rafaello admitted curtly, stabbing a couple of buttons.

With a slight lurch the lift set off downward again, while Glory smoothed shaking hands down her rucked sweater. She could not bring herself to look at him. It was one of those moments when intense mortification and essential honesty combined to prevent her from coming up with a single face-saving excuse. Her lips burning from the heat of his, her trembling body still struggling to come down from the heights of anticipation he had contrived to fire within seconds of touching her, she felt shattered.

'We'll go back to my apartment,' Rafaello breathed thickly.

Sensing that lunch would not be Rafaello's most pressing goal, Glory reddened to the roots of her hair with shame. 'Nothing doing. I'm going home. I told you that. This was an accident—'

'An...accident?' Rafaello repeated in thunderous disbelief.

'Like when you take your eyes off the road and *crash*!' Glory stressed shakily, almost being eaten alive by the strength of her own self-loathing.

The lift doors swept back with an electronic beep of warning, exposing them to all onlookers. There was a crush of bodies waiting outside but their impatient surge forward was arrested by the sight of the male within. A sea of wildly curious faces stared in at Rafaello and Glory.

Glory lurched into frantic motion. She pushed her way through the stilled crowd and then raced across the busy ground-floor foyer for the exit doors. She ran a good half of the way back to the train station and then, winded and barely able to catch her breath, was forced to halt her mad flight and walk instead.

However, the sense of panic and severe embarrassment induced by what she had allowed to happen between herself and Rafaello was in no way lessened. How *could* she have behaved like that? One minute telling him she had only come back to give him a piece of her mind, the next winding herself round him like the weakest of choking vines. Talk about handing out conflicting signals!

CHAPTER THREE

THE following day Glory had an early shift at the factory and then finished work early, as was the norm on a Friday afternoon.

Feeling exhausted, she trudged up the stairs to her top-floor bedsit. She had her key in the door before she actually noticed the slip of paper stuck to the scarred wood. 'Urgent,' ran the message in the girl next door's handwriting. 'Phone your dad!'

Her heart in her mouth at the thought of what those four words might mean, Glory clattered back down the stairs again to use the coinbox phone in the hall.

Her father answered her call almost immediately. 'Is that you, Glory?'

'What is it? What's happened?' she prompted breathlessly.

'The police arrived first thing this morning with a search warrant.'

'A s-search warrant?' Glory stammered in horror.

'They found that stolen snuff box hidden in our fuel shed,' Archie Little told her heavily. 'Sam was arrested. The police have charged him, but he didn't do it. I *know* he didn't do it!'

As Glory absorbed what her father was telling her, shock chilled her skin to the temperature of ice. 'Sam was arrested...and charged?'

'His best mate is the one who did the stealing,' he asserted bitterly. 'When Sam came to me for help during that party Joe was with him, but he insisted on staying outside. When I left the cottage to go up and turf their mates out of the Park I saw Joe coming out of the shed—'

'Oh, Dad...' Glory mumbled sickly, her heart sinking like a stone.

'I wondered what the kid had been doing but I was too keen to get that party stopped to waste time asking him. But Joe must've panicked and hidden the box then. But who's going to believe that when it was found in *our* shed?' Archie Little demanded on the rising note of a man already taxed beyond his endurance level. 'What are we going to do, Glory? I don't know what to do or where to turn now—'

'I'll sort something out,' Glory heard herself insist with forced confidence. 'Tell Sam I'm thinking of him and that I believe in him—'

'How are you going to sort out anything? It's too late,' her father groaned, and she could hear the thickness of tears and the defeat in his response. 'The solicitor says we just have to wait until it comes to court.'

'Trust me...I'll arrange something, I *swear* I will. Don't let Sam get too upset about this,' Glory warned, because her kid brother was an emotional boy and now she was worried sick. Suppose he ran away or, even worse, became even more depressed and did something foolish? She shivered. Her father was not the rock that a scared teenager needed for support, nor the best person to persuade Sam that they could fight to prove his innocence.

Only when Glory came off the phone did she discover that she was shaking like a leaf. Momentarily she closed her eyes in anguish. She could have saved Sam from the ordeal of being arrested and charged. But now that the forces of law and order had got involved, was it even possible that the theft charge could be dropped? And even if it was possible, would Rafaello now be willing to do it?

She lifted out her purse and searched for the phone number she had used forty-eight hours earlier to contact Rafaello's London office and ask for her appointment. She got passed through to his secretary, but there the trail as such threatened to go cold. Rafaello was not available, she was told starchily.

'Has he gone abroad?' Glory pressed fearfully. 'Look, this is very urgent. I really need to know where he is.'

'Mr Grazzini is at his country house and I'm afraid I'm not able to give you either the address or the phone number. However, I will pass on your message—'

'No, please don't do that!' Glory interrupted in dismay, thinking that forewarning of her change of heart might only harden his. In another mood she might have smiled at the secretary's mistake in mentioning Rafaello's whereabouts. Naturally the woman had no idea that Glory would know exactly where that country house was situated.

An element of surprise might be the only thing she had going for her, Glory reflected in desperation as she yanked out her travel bag. She would catch the train down to Montague Park and try to see Rafaello before she went to see her family. What else could she do? Leave Sam facing theft charges? But would Rafaello even *listen* to her now?

After her senseless behaviour the afternoon before Glory knew that Rafaello would be furious with her. Her second visit to his office and her wild response to that steamy embrace, followed by her equally sudden flight, had been madness. Even with the best will in the world, she knew she could never explain why she had gone back while still maintaining that she had no intention of accepting his offer. If she couldn't explain that to herself, how could she possibly hope to explain it to him?

Zipping up her bag, she looked at herself in the mirror and almost had a heart attack! Her hair was falling down in messy strands from an unglamorous pony-tail. Her pale, anxious face was bare of make-up and her jeans and shirt were hardly of the ilk calculated to persuade a man that she was worth sacrificing a principle for. And, where principles were concerned, Rafaello could make a person feel distinctly uncomfortable. He had said the offer would be

closed if she did not take it up in the time frame he had
set. So if she was to persuade him otherwise she would
have to look good, look *seductive*…?

Not a challenge Glory had ever taken on before, when
her greatest need had always been to find one special man
who would see her as a person rather than a sexual challenge and a trophy. Already painfully aware that her full-
lipped face, blonde hair and hourglass shape encouraged
men to assume that she would be an easy lay, Glory never
wore provocative clothes. But provocative was the look required, wasn't it? Reminding herself of her kid brother's
current plight, she left her bedsit to knock on her neigh-
bour's door.

Tania, a small, bubbly brunette, currently working nights
in a busy city bar, opened her door. 'Glory…did you get
my message?'

'Yes, thanks. Look, I was wondering, would you let me
borrow one of your clubbing outfits?' Glory asked hesi-
tantly.

Tania surveyed her with an exaggerated dropped jaw.

'I'd be really careful with it,' Glory promised in a humble tone.

'Are you the woman who told me you wouldn't be seen
dead flashing your legs in a short skirt just to give some
sick bloke a cheap thrill?'

Glory reddened and nodded slowly.

'Are you the same woman who told me boobs were made
to be covered, not put out like cut-price fruit on a stall?'

Glory winced at that second reminder and nodded again
in guilty confirmation.

Tania gave her cringing visitor a hugely amused grin and
let Glory in. 'So tell me…who's the guy you're hanging
up your combat trousers and workman's boots for?'

Glory paled and thought. 'A challenge?'

'I *love* a challenge!' Tania threw wide the door of her

crammed wardrobe. 'Trust me, Glory. Now that you've owned up to your desperation, I'll be your best pal.'

Three-quarters of an hour later Glory studied her transformed appearance in her own room. A frilly pink top hugged her lush bosom, and she had had to squeeze into the stretchy short pink skirt with its racy split. Her stiletto-heeled shoes had only two tiny narrow satin bands studded with diamanté to hold in her feet. Above one ankle she now sported a fashionable henna transfer tattoo in an oriental design. Tattoos drive men *wild* Tania had assured her. Glory had wondered out loud whether some males might prefer greater subtlety. But Tania it had to be admitted, had far more experience, and had said that at heart men were one and all the same: they were just slaves to their hormones every time.

'You're gonna stop the traffic. Next time we go out together, you put on your combat trousers and boots again.' Tania warned her, smoothing the shining mane of honey-blonde hair which hung halfway down Glory's narrow back. 'I couldn't stick this amount of competition. I'd be so jealous, I'd never speak to you again.'

'No problem. I don't like looking like this…not that I'm not grateful,' Glory added hurriedly as she pulled on her raincoat.

'I hope he's worth the effort—'

'*He* probably thinks he is.' Glory set off for the bus that would take her to the train.

Shortly after seven that evening, Glory finally reached the imposing gates of Montague Park and contemplated the mile-long driveway that stretched before her.

Chafed by the diamanté straps, her feet were already in agony. And, in truth, she did not actually *want* to arrive at her destination. Or that ghastly moment when she would have to tell Rafaello that he had won and that she would be his for as long as he wanted it that way. While she cringed for herself and grovelled, she would also have the added torment of knowing that he was enjoying every minute of her major climbdown.

Twenty minutes later she reached the grand front doors of the superb Georgian mansion and hit the bell.

The housekeeper, Maud Belper, gazed out at her in astonished recognition. 'Glory?'

'I'd be really grateful if you wouldn't mention to my dad that you saw me here,' Glory whispered guiltily, sidling in past the older woman, who had known her since childhood. 'Is Mr Grazzini home?'

'Would that be Mr Benito or Mr Rafaello?' Maud enquired, deciding that two could play the mystery game of mutual ignorance.

'Rafaello,' Glory mumbled, her colour heightening.

'Let me take your coat—'

Glory clutched her coat to her. 'No…no, thanks. I've got a cold coming on and I'm feeling the chill.'

'Mr Grazzini's in the library.'

Glory nodded and listened to the housekeeper's steps retreat at a tellingly slow pace.

Leaving her travel bag behind, she limped over to the library door on her poor, tortured feet and undid the belt on her raincoat. She felt like a flasher. Suppose Rafaello laughed? Suppose she did genuinely look as trashy and silly as she feared that she did? This is for *Sam*, she reminded herself, and on the spur of that she walked into the room, paused and discarded the coat in almost the same movement. He could only interpret her announced arrival and her vampish appearance in one way. And, if he took that hint, hopefully she wouldn't have to grovel quite so much.

Talking on the phone over by the window, Rafaello froze as though Glory had burst in waving a hand grenade. He blinked. He looked again, kept on looking. Stunned dark golden eyes started afresh at the crown of her honey-blonde head, worked slowly down over her taut but beautiful face and back over the full pouting thrust of her breasts as delineated in skintight pink. There he seemed to pause to take a much needed break and he breathed in audibly before meeting the challenge of proceeding further in a downward direction.

Glory stood there like a martyr tied to the stake with a face hotter than any flames could have provoked. She could feel every ragged breath struggling past her convulsed throat as the tension rose. Staying still and silent was the hardest thing she had ever done. He had forced her to reduce herself to the level of a sex object desperate to sell herself to the highest bidder, and her pride was crushed.

Rafaello had trouble dragging his attention from the well-defined curve of her hips, but when he reached her legs he appeared to be even more challenged to keep his intent appraisal moving. Finally his scrutiny screamed to a halt above the slender ankle displaying the henna transfer tattoo.

Suddenly he flashed his smouldering eyes back up to her severely strained features. An aristocratic black brow was elevated. 'What *is* this? A pantomime in which you star as the sex bomb?'

Glory had never been very confident that Rafaello would be a slave to his hormones as Tania had forecast, for Rafaello had a natural stubborn streak that rejoiced in never doing exactly what was expected of him. A 'pantomime'? She shrivelled with embarrassment at his use of that particular word. His sardonic response annihilated her where she stood.

Stepping painfully off one foot onto the other, striving to spread the agony of her complaining toes, Glory stooped. In a harried movement she snatched up her coat and dived back into its concealing folds. Once again she had made a total fool of herself, she reflected in choked mortification. Scorching tears lashed the backs of her eyes so hard she had to widen them and focus on a point over his shoulder to keep them from falling.

'No, of course I am not talking to *you*,' Rafaello breathed with chilling cool to the excusably confused and unfortunate person he had been speaking to on the phone when she first entered and whose invisible listening presence he had briefly forgotten. 'I have a visitor. I'll call you back.'

While he spoke Glory watched him. A powerful feeling of torment and tragedy was now assailing her already ragged nerves. Why had she torn off her raincoat in that utterly stupid way? She had been terrified that she would lose her nerve at the last moment. She had hoped to strike an impression of being cool, even rather amused and scornful, but fully in control of events. She had failed: he thought she looked ridiculous. But there *he* was, the very image of enviable cool and sophistication in a superbly tailored dark suit that was probably the ultimate in Italian style.

Rafaello cast aside the receiver. Dark, deep-set eyes hooded, he scanned Glory as she hugged her coat as if it was the only thing standing between her and total nudity. 'I'm waiting for an explanation.'

'What do you want me to say?' Glory asked jaggedly, her throat closing over, her wide, over-bright eyes staring a hole into the middle distance. She had looked enough at him. That bold masculine face in profile, the shadow his lush black lashes cast on one high cheekbone, the arrogant nose, the wide, sexy mouth. Even half a view of him made her heart race and set butterflies dancing in her tummy.

'OK...' Rafaello drawled in the silken tone of a male taking up a challenge without hesitation. 'Yesterday you raced back to my office and fell into my arms—'

'I did not *fall* into your arms, I was grabbed—' Glory squeezed out between gritted teeth.

Rafaello ignored that contradiction. 'If I hadn't called time I do believe we would've had sex in the lift—'

'Speak for yourself!' Glory launched at him in strong chagrin. 'I don't behave like that—'

'Don't you?' Rafaello vented a derisive laugh. 'When you burst in here I thought some maniac had decided to treat me to a strippergram!'

'A...what?' Glory gasped in dismay.

'Dressed like that you look like a cheap little scrubber.' Rafaello skimmed her a brooding scrutiny and his hard sensual mouth twisted. 'Not my style; a definite turn-off.'

Veiling her stricken gaze, Glory dropped her head and gulped in sustaining air like a drowning swimmer. Hurt and humiliated by that blunt assessment, she had to bite back the impulsive words rising to her lips. She could not afford to antagonise Rafaello when her brother's whole future rested in his hands. A taut silence stretched while she fought an almost overwhelming urge to tell him what he could do with his uninvited opinions. So she had got the outfit wrong. But then, what had he expected? Some classy designer number? Never had the gap between her world and his seemed as great as it did at that moment.

'Since you're lousy at getting to the point, isn't it fortunate that I can work out exactly what you're doing here?' Rafaello remarked drily.

Prompted, Glory glanced up, her lovely face tense with strain. Brilliant dark eyes slammed into hers and she trembled, her mouth running dry. 'I'm certain that Sam didn't steal that snuff box, but I know things don't look good for him and that it'll be very hard to prove that he's innocent. You did say that if you got the box back you might consider *not* pressing charges—'

'Only I was talking about it being returned voluntarily,' Rafaello contradicted with chilling cool. 'Not found during a police search.'

Glory had not really had any hope that he would not make that distinction but she had felt that she ought to try out that angle. 'All right...' she breathed unevenly. 'So if you can still get the charges dropped, well...I'll do whatever you want.'

Rafaello strolled soundlessly over to the windows before swinging back round to look at her again, his lean, strong face intent. 'I can have the theft charge withdrawn but how do I know that you'll respect your side of the agreement?'

At the news that the charge of theft *could* still be withdrawn, a little colour eased back into Glory's complexion. But she was strung so high with tension that even her knees had begun to wobble. 'Whatever you think of me, I'm not a cheat or a liar.'

Rafaello scanned her with unreadable dark eyes. 'My father certainly had no grounds for complaint after the bargain he struck with you. Unless I'm very much mistaken, it *has* been five years since you set foot on Grazzini land. You can't have seen much of your father and your brother since then.'

Was that actually a hint of censure that she was hearing? Sam and Glory talked on the phone most weeks. For the first couple of years she had lived in Gloucester with her father's sister and she had often seen her family. But when her aunt passed away, Glory had had to move further north to find employment, and inevitably the frequency of their meetings had declined. No longer could Glory feel that she was as close to her younger brother as she had once been. Acknowledging that truth, she felt hugely bitter at the damage that Benito Grazzini had cruelly inflicted on her small family circle.

'Living a couple of hundred miles away hasn't exactly been a help,' Glory said defensively. 'We don't all have limos and private jets to get around in.'

'But you will have for as long as you're with me.' Losing interest in the subject that he himself had raised, Rafaello studied her with a reflective all-male intensity that sent fresh pink flying into her cheeks. 'You can take your coat off. I assume you're staying tonight.'

Glory froze. 'Tonight?'

Rafaello dealt her a lazy mocking smile. 'Were you waiting for me to schedule in a date for next month?'

'But tonight…for goodness' sake!' Glory was seriously challenged to maintain any form of cool when she realised how soon he was expecting her to meet and deliver on the terms of their agreement. 'After this I was planning to go and see Dad and Sam and surprise them.'

'Surprise me instead,' Rafaello invited softly. 'If your family aren't expecting you, you'll find yourself facing some awkward questions. I'll have the theft charge dropped and I'll personally inform your father of that decision this evening.'

'That's great,' Glory told him gratefully. 'But—'

'You will be flying out to Corfu tomorrow,' Rafaello cut in quietly.

'Tomorrow? Corfu?' Her blue eyes had widened to their fullest extent. He was expecting her to go abroad? 'Are you crazy? I have a job, a home and a whole bunch of stuff to sort out before I can go *anywhere*—'

'I'll have someone clear your bedsit, settle any final bills and inform your landlord and your employer that you're not coming back. It's not a problem.'

'Well, it is a problem for me. I can do all those things for myself within a couple of days,' Glory argued in a flustered but insistent undertone. 'But if you're expecting me to go abroad with you I want to see my family tonight.'

'If you walk out on me one more time you can forget about walking back in again.'

The silence shimmered like the menacing quiet before a storm. Chilled by that cold threat that cut unmercifully through her every argument, Glory studied Rafaello in genuine shock.

Rafaello gazed back at her with hard dark eyes that had no shade of lighter emotional gold.

'Why are you being like this?' Glory muttered helplessly.

'I've surrendered every way I can but it's still not enough for you.'

'Don't exaggerate, *cara*.' With complete cool, Rafaello reached out to loosen her tight grip on her raincoat and fold her taut fingers into the hold of his. 'I just don't want there to be any misunderstandings between us. I'm calling the shots. What else did you expect?'

At the warmth of his hands on hers, Glory trembled. She gazed up into eyes dark as midnight but she had already lost his direct attention. Her raincoat had fallen open. His lowered gaze was welded to the exposed curves of her pouting breasts. A shocking stab of hurt travelled through her. 'You said…you *said* I looked like a cheap little scrubber in this get-up, so why are you looking at me like that?'

'Intellect aside, I'm still a red-blooded male with all the usual painfully predictable reactions.' His smouldering dark golden scrutiny skimmed back up to her self-conscious face. 'You're no longer that guileless teenager who burned me up with the lure of her supposed innocence, but that's a plus now. I want an experienced lover in my bed, a woman who can satisfy my every need.'

That admission made Glory stiffen. She dropped her head to hide the hectic flush in her cheeks. She was not ashamed of being a virgin, but nor was she prepared to take the risk of telling him the truth. Suppose he changed his mind about the arrangement he had offered her? A male, who was only interested in his own sexual pleasure would naturally prefer a woman who could match his own expertise between the sheets. And by the sounds of it, Rafaello had pretty *high* expectations. However, he was destined to meet with a major disappointment in that department. But to her way of thinking, there was a certain natural rough justice to that reality. Rafaello would get exactly what he deserved.

'I think the only reason you want me is because I turned

you down five years ago,' Glory said before she could think better of that leading comment.

Lean fingers found her chin and turned up her eyes to encounter the scorching gold of his own. 'You could be right, but then I never really turned up the heat, did I?'

'Didn't you?' Her own voice sounded slightly strangled as he let that controlling hand drift down to the base of her spine instead.

All of a sudden even catching her breath and clearing her dry throat was a challenge. The tension in the atmosphere was electrifying. Her heart was racing like a trapped bird inside her ribcage and she was aware of Rafaello's potent masculinity with every fibre of her being.

'I was playing a waiting game,' Rafaello confided huskily. 'But now I don't need to wait.'

He was going to touch her and she wanted him to touch her. Indeed, she could hardly *wait* for him to touch her, she registered in dismay. But even the shame that followed that acknowledgement could not still the insidious awakening of her own body. She was painfully conscious of the swelling heaviness of her breasts and the aching sensitivity of their rosy peaks but most of all of the betraying surge of moist heat at the very heart of her.

He urged her closer and her nostrils flared on the heady familiarity of his scent. The faint aroma of aftershave underscored by warm male. She trembled, wanting, needing, suddenly strung up to such a height of hunger, she was dizzy with it. And then he took her mouth and kissed her with sensual probing intensity and it was as if her heart stopped on the unbearable sweetness of that sensation before thundering on faster and wilder in beat than ever before.

'Imagine saying no to this, *cara...*' Rafaello murmured thickly, lifting his arrogant dark head while she struggled for breath and the independent strength to hold herself upright instead of holding on to him for support.

Glory was devastated by her own sheer longing to be back in his arms again. 'Stop teasing me…'

'Is this what you call teasing?' Shimmering golden eyes scanned her with predatory amusement. 'Slow and seductive not what you're used to, *cara mia*?'

In the grip of that passionate yearning, her quivering body no longer felt like her own. She gave way to her own frustration. She reached up and dragged his mouth back down to hers again. As her seeking fingers laced into his luxuriant black hair, he loosed a sound somewhere between a laugh and a groan. But in response he let his tongue probe deep between her lips in an explicit penetration that made her shiver with helpless anticipation against his hard, muscular frame. Closing his hands to her hips, he lifted her off her feet.

'Rafaello…?' Glory was taken aback when he settled her down on top of the antique mahogany desk.

'You're too short to be fully accessible upright,' he mocked, curling his hand into the fall of her honey-blonde mane and then letting his fingertips skim appreciatively through the glossy strands. '*Santo cielo!* Your hair feels like pure silk…'

Before she could even guess his intention, he had parted her knees and drawn her right to the edge of the desk. Then he eased his hands beneath her hips and lifted her back to him in a much more intimate connection than had been possible while she had been standing. Her legs apart and left to dangle either side of his lean, powerful length as he moved into the space he had created for himself, Glory felt suddenly out of her depth and vulnerable. As she fought to force her stretchy skirt back down over her exposed thighs, even the heat of her own shivering hunger was incapable of silencing the alarm bells of panic his behaviour was rousing.

'What are you doing?' Glory exclaimed.

Rafaello looked down at her with stunning dark golden

eyes, a frownline etched between his winged dark brows. 'What's wrong?'

'What's wrong?' Glory demanded incredulously half an octave higher. 'You're expecting me to carry on with you on top of a desk and you're asking *me* what's wrong?'

Rafaello stilled as if she had thrown a stop switch. Lush black lashes dropped down to conceal his gaze.

'Because cavorting on desks is *out!*' Glory told him fiercely, the fear that he was trying to make a fool of her trammelling through her in an enervating wave. 'I've met some real full-on creeps in my time but even they didn't try to jump me on a desk—'

'Is that a fact?' Rafaello breathed not quite levelly, apparently transfixed by her frantic efforts to drag the hem of her skirt down over her thighs. Helpfully he stepped back so that she could lock her knees together again and achieve that feat.

'Yes, that is a fact,' Glory told him chokily, tears roughening her voice as her distress climbed in direct proportion to her embarrassment. 'I want respect. I want boundaries to this "anything you want" stuff—'

'I get the feeling that, on your terms, the desk is the absolute outer limits,' Rafaello murmured in a taut undertone that shook slightly, his Italian accent thicker than she had ever heard it.

'It's a question of what's decent.'

'You're not very adventurous, are you?'

'Not in lifts or on desks,' Glory agreed shakily, sliding off the wooden surface in haste and smoothing her rucked clothing down with trembling hands.

'I wasn't actually *planning* to consummate our agreement on the library desk—'

Too self-conscious to look at him, her cheeks hotter than hellfire, Glory shrugged a slight shoulder in a jerky, defensive motion. 'How was I supposed to know what you were planning? You embarrassed me—'

'Tell me, do you know what foreplay is?'

If Glory had been feeling overheated before he said that in the charged tone of a male trying hard not to laugh at what he obviously found amusing, her temperature hit boiling point in receipt of that mocking enquiry.

'I do know you're not talking about golf, if that's what you mean!' she launched back at him angrily, bright blue eyes sparking fierily. 'But I'm not here to be the butt of your smart-mouth comments, Rafaello Grazzini—'

'And you're not here to cavort on my desk either. Sorry, couldn't resist it, *cara*,' Rafaello drawled, lean, strong face expressionless. 'I think what we need here is a list—'

'A…what?'

'Of places where sexual activity is forbidden. And, while we're on the subject, possibly you ought to consider throwing in news of any other strong aversions before I share a bed with you.'

Encountering those brilliant, beautiful dark eyes, Glory paled. 'You think this is funny, don't you?'

'No, I'm fascinated. In my entire experience of women, I have never had a conversation quite like this,' Rafaello assured her, smooth as silk. 'It looks as if your mother is going to have the last laugh on me after all. And please do not take that comment as any form of insult to her memory.'

Glory swallowed hard. Her throat thickened. She felt more like bursting into tears. Just then she did not need the reminder of her late mother. Not on the very night she was being expected to abandon those principles. She saw that nerves and shyness had made her overreact to an unfamiliar and seemingly threatening situation. He had only wanted to kiss her, maybe touch her a little. But she had thrown a three-act tragedy and made an ass of herself in the process.

'I'm glad I've given you a laugh,' she muttered, cut to the bone.

Rafaello released his breath on a slight hiss and reached

for her tightly knotted fingers to urge her back to him. She moved only when the pressure got too much to withstand. With a rueful groan, he murmured, 'I wasn't laughing—'

'You *were*,' she mumbled tightly, the tears threatening.

'You're wearing a real in-your-face sexy outfit. I didn't think a woman who dressed like that would take fright quite so easily,' Rafaello admitted above her downbent head.

'I did *not* take fright,' Glory bit out in a driven tone, picturing a panicking Victorian spinster screaming on a stool at the sight of a mouse.

'OK…you took offence, but it's over,' Rafaello rephrased in his deep, husky drawl. 'Go on upstairs. After I've called your father, I'll join you.'

Glory froze, all her nervous tension returning. 'Where?'

'In my bedroom. Of course, you've never been upstairs. I'll take you up—'

'No, just tell me where,' Glory interrupted tautly.

A phone began to ring. Rafaello released an imprecation in his own language, hesitated and then strode impatiently back over to the desk. 'It's my private line. I should answer it in case it's something important.'

'Where?' she prompted again, grabbing up her coat and sticking her arms into the sleeves.

'First door off the main landing. *Stay*,' Rafaello urged as he reached for the phone and, studying her, he surprised her by stretching out an inviting hand.

Glory hovered. A smile curved his wide, expressive mouth, a smile full of heartbreaking charm. The smile that had once enslaved her heart as efficiently as chains. Her heartbeat quickening, she found herself returning to his side and reaching out to clasp that outstretched hand.

Rafaello's grip on her fingers tightened. She glanced up, saw the frownline indented between his brows and listened to him talk in what sounded like Italian. His tone was questioning and a faint look of irritation narrowed his incisive gaze. He replaced the receiver and released her hand again.

'Fate seems to have it in for us tonight,' Rafaello breathed with a wry look. 'That was my father.'

'Oh…?' Glory tautened with unease.

'He's staying in London with friends this weekend. But he's just informed me that he'll be here in ten minutes to discuss some urgent matter that he insists cannot wait until tomorrow.' Raking lean brown fingers through his thick black hair, Rafaello sighed. 'Perhaps now that the novelty has worn off, he's finding retirement a challenge. But he did sound troubled and that isn't like him.'

'I should clear off down to the cottage and see my own family,' Glory proffered in an eager rush at the prospect of escape.

'*No.*' It was one word said with quiet force but it stilled her in her tracks.

'I don't want to bump into your father, Rafaello.' She almost told him that one Grazzini at a time was quite sufficient for her.

'You'll be quite safe in my bedroom. Benito hasn't tucked me in at night since I was five years old,' Rafaello informed her with sardonic bite. 'But, for what it's worth, I don't feel any need to hide you. Join us. He's going to know about us sooner or later anyway.'

Benito Grazzini would be astonished and angry to find her under his son's roof, and Glory had not the slightest desire to meet the forceful older man again. However, Rafaello's invitation shook her. 'That doesn't mean I want to be around when he finds out—'

'Coward,' Rafaello mocked, leaning down to capture her tense lips and extract a hungry kiss.

'I'll be more comfortable upstairs,' Glory protested, her reddened mouth tingling from the effect of that sensual collision and her feet inexplicably welded to the spot.

Rafaello gave her a wolfish grin. 'So will I be…'

The reminder of the true situation between them made her flush and head in haste for the door.

CHAPTER FOUR

GLORY picked up her bag where she had left it sitting in the big, elegant hall. Pausing only to slip off the diamanté sandals which had scored deep welts across her toes, Glory headed for the grand staircase as quietly and quickly as she could.

But luck was not on Glory's side. Maud Belper appeared from behind the green baize door below the stairs that led to the kitchen quarters. 'You're staying here, then?'

Hot, guilty, embarrassed pink from throat to brow, Glory gave a reluctant nod of confirmation.

'Your father's a mild man, Glory. It takes a lot to upset him but I honestly think he would lose his head with Mr Rafaello over this.'

Glory stilled and tried to act dignified. 'I'm a grown woman, not a kid.'

'It wouldn't be about that, love.' The grey-haired older woman frowned, her rounded good-natured face troubled. 'I ought to be minding my own business and I'm no tittle-tattle. But I just feel I should warn you that you're getting into a situation you don't really understand.'

Having made that far from reassuring and deeply mysterious statement, the housekeeper went back through the green baize door without another word. Glory hastened on up the stairs in craven flight. What on earth was Maud Belper talking about? *What* situation? And why, when she was about to let herself down a bucketful with Rafaello, did there have to be a talkative witness lecturing on the sidelines?

Glory hurtled in through the first door off the main landing, thrust the door shut behind her and fumbled for the light. Then she understood why Rafaello had such a big office. It was only what he was used to, she decided, scanning the huge bedroom with inquisitive eyes. A bed the size of a football pitch sat dead-centre. Skittish as a racehorse, she averted her attention from it and studied the remainder of the elegant furniture. It was a very beautiful room. The pastel rug on the floor, the subdued wallpaper and the long curtains did not match, yet somehow the overall effect was subtle and very classy, she acknowledged. Then she caught a glimpse of herself in a tall dressing mirror, and stiffened in dismay.

Unsubtle, too bold, Glory decided as she scrutinised her own reflection with newly critical eyes. She wondered how a skirt and top that had looked so pretty and feminine on Tania could look so very different on her. Of course, Tania was a brunette and a little less curvy. It had stabbed Glory to the heart when Rafaello told her that she looked cheap but she could see now that, whether she liked it or not, he had been right.

Catching sight of the transfer design above her ankle, she wrinkled her nose and went into the imposing *en suite* with its marble-set sinks. Stripping off her tights, she ran some water and tried to wash off the fake tattoo. The transfer was more resistant than she had expected. As she frowned down at her leg it occurred to her that she should be more worried by her own behaviour than about how she looked to *him*.

Here she was, selling herself like a commodity for Sam's sake. Well, not entirely for Sam's sake, Glory adjusted guiltily. There was this dreadful enemy part of her which wanted Rafaello Grazzini any way she could get him. She was deeply ashamed of that truth but too essentially honest to deny it. He had driven her into an arrangement that was going to break her heart and smash her pride forever.

She was soft where feelings were concerned. She always had been. She got attached to people. She had never quite managed to detach herself from him. And why not? They had had six enchanted weeks together before everything went wrong, and during those weeks, he had treated her better than any man she had met before or since. She hadn't had to fight for her life or deal with him getting into an all-male sulk at having his attentions refused. There had been a kind of teasing quality to his approaches, she recalled abstractedly. Only there had been nothing teasing about the manner in which Rafaello had arranged her on that desk downstairs...

Not knowing what was likely to happen next and hugely conscious that she did not want to experience intimacy for the first time on a desk in a very well-lit room, she had panicked. *Really* panicked, she conceded ruefully. Only true panic could possibly have snatched her from the intoxicating excitement of Rafaello's mouth on hers. But it shocked her that after five years he could touch her again and make her want him like that. It scared her even more that, in her heart of hearts, she still could not credit that Rafaello would actually make her his mistress.

But why not? When Glory was sixteen, and she had first met Rafaello face-to-face, he had behaved more like a protective big brother. Still barefoot, she wandered back into the bedroom but her thoughts were miles away. Having a huge crush on Rafaello had not stopped Glory from wanting a boyfriend of her own because all her school friends had been dating by then. She had believed that nothing would ever come of her dreams about Rafaello Grazzini. After all, not only had she never even had the opportunity to speak to him, but she and Rafaello had also lived and moved in different worlds.

Unfortunately, Talitha Little had refused to allow her daughter to go out to bars or clubs or to start dating. Almost inevitably, in her last term at school Glory had rebelled and gone behind her mother's back. Her best friend had set her up with one of her older brother's mates and had invited her to stay over that night so that she could get dressed up and come home late. A whole crowd of them had gone to a local bar and Glory's date, Tim, a smooth-talking twenty-five-year-old, had introduced her to alcohol.

'Hey, look who's here,' her friend had whispered, nudging her in the ribs halfway through that evening. 'Talk about slumming!'

Rafaello had been standing by the bar with a couple of other young men, their designer casuals marking them out as more than a cut above the majority of the clientele. Glory had not been able to take her eyes from him, for she had never seen him that close before. Indeed, most of her sightings of Rafaello had been when he drove past her in his sports car while she was walking home after getting off the school bus. Although he had been known to offer other people lifts on wet days, he had never once offered her one.

Even though she had been staring a hole in him, it had been a shock when Rafaello looked directly at her for the first time. She remembered going all red in the face but not being able to drag her gaze from the magnetic spell of his lustrous dark eyes.

'I think you're in with a chance there all right,' her irrepressible friend had hissed. 'It's a shame you're stuck with Tim.'

But Tim had gone to play darts at the other end of the crowded bar and Glory, emboldened by the unfamiliar effects of alcohol on her system, sat there with her entire attention shamelessly focused on Rafaello, flirting like mad with her eyes. She saw his companions noticing her and commenting and thrilled in her naïvety to the belief that if she was being discussed the commentary could only be an appreciative one. In that over-excited state, it was really not that big a surprise when, on her passage back from the cloakroom, Rafaello intercepted her.

'Would you like to go for a drive in my Porsche?' he murmured huskily.

Thrilled to death by that invitation, it could not be said that she played hard to get. 'When?'

'Now. Just follow me outside.'

And, just like that, she did. She had a little difficulty walking in a straight line across the car park.

'Not the most loyal of girlfriends, are you?' Rafaello remarked.

'I only met him tonight,' Glory hastened to inform him. 'You recognised me, didn't you?'

'Oh, yes…you're not easily missed.'

He unlocked the Porsche and settled her inside first with the kind of well-bred good manners that thrilled her. And while she was sitting there frantically trying to think of something witty to say, he drove her *home*.

'What…why are you bringing me back here?' Glory demanded, aghast at the sight of her parental home. 'I'm supposed to be staying at my friend's house tonight. I can't go home dressed like this, not when I've been drinking either… I thought you were taking me for a drive!'

'I just did—'

'No, but *I* thought—'

'You're not capable of thinking anything right now. Your date was deliberately getting you drunk. You shouldn't be drinking under age, particularly when you're not mature enough for adult company—'

'What are you talking about?' Glory screeched at him in anguish.

'You just walked out of that bar with me and got into my car. Don't you realise how dangerous it is for a woman to behave like that? You don't have the wit of a newborn baby. The safest place for you is home—'

'My mother will *kill* me!' she launched at him in complete panic.

'I'll have a word with her.' Thrusting open the driver's door, Rafaello cut short the dialogue.

Glory burst into floods of tears. He extracted her from

his passenger seat only with difficulty. 'I just couldn't stand by watching that slimeball filling you up with booze,' he breathed impatiently. 'Surely you realise how he was planning to end the evening?'

'You let me think that *you*—'

'You're out of bounds, Glory. You're only sixteen.'

'You were looking at me like you fancied me!' she condemned tearfully.

'Easiest way to get you out of there, and it wasn't difficult…you're a very beautiful girl—'

'Do you think so?' she asked him pathetically, and he laughed and her heart had gone crazy—but then her mother opened the front door.

Although Talitha Little had a hot temper, she had not said that much that night. The next morning over breakfast, while Glory was nursing a vicious hangover and being forced to explain herself, her mother had given her an odd little smile and had remarked that she was quite sure that Glory had learned her lesson well. Glory had spent the whole of that summer mulling over every word that Rafaello had said to her, and, appalled by the effect that alcohol had had on her usual caution, she had never touched it since then.

Emerging from those memories, Glory glanced at her watch and realised that she had already been upstairs for an hour. How could the same male who had protected her from her own juvenile stupidity be the same guy she was dealing with now? Was Benito Grazzini still with Rafaello? Glory crept out of the bedroom and crossed the landing to peer down into the hall. When the library door opened she backed away. She watched Rafaello and his father, a big barrel-chested man with silver hair, move to the front door together in silence. Benito Grazzini walked out and then abruptly turned to speak and to spread his hands in what looked curiously like an emotive appeal for understanding. Glory was shocked by the expression on the older man's face. He looked ravaged, almost distraught. But Rafaello's profile was taut and grim. He made no response. After a moment Benito let his hands fall back to his sides in an attitude of weary defeat. Shoulders bowed, the older man turned and walked slowly and heavily out to the waiting limo gleaming beneath the outside lights. Rafaello thrust the door shut again.

'Rafaello?' Glory called down, for she could not silence herself. 'What's happened? What's wrong?'

He froze in surprise and then threw back his dark head and looked up to where she stood at the head of the staircase. His lean, strong face was shuttered. 'How long have you been up there?'

'Only a minute. I saw your father leave. He seemed upset—'

Rafaello lifted a broad shoulder in a faint shrug of indifference, but he was unusually pale. His expressive mouth clenched hard and his dark eyes were cold. '*Did* he?'

As he mounted the stairs to draw level with her Glory coloured with discomfiture. Obviously he had had a disagreement with the older man. But then, two such powerful personalities might well have regular differences of opinion and she could hardly blame him for snubbing her: it was none of her business. Or *was* it? Was it possible that the argument might have related to her? Before she could think better of asking such a question, she said, 'Did you tell your father that I was here? Is that what caused the trouble between you?'

'Hardly,' Rafaello drawled with detached and dismissive cool. 'But my plans have changed. I know it's getting late but I'm going to have you driven back to Birmingham. Something rather more important than my libido has cropped up and I need to deal with it now.'

Wholly unprepared for that announcement, Glory stiffened in astonishment. She turned away, her face burning with sudden mortification. One minute he wanted her, the next he didn't, and she was being dismissed like a casual employee. Yet it was so foolish of her to be feeling like that in the circumstances. She ought to be delighted and relieved, she told herself. 'I'll get my bag.'

'I'll send a car to pick you up on Monday around noon. I'll need your address—'

She hesitated but did not turn back. 'Are you still planning to let Sam know tonight that he doesn't have to worry about that theft charge any more?'

A tense and unexpected silence stretched and, with a frown, she turned her head to look at him again.

'Yes,' Rafaello breathed with a grim look etched on his lean, dark features. 'Yes, you can bet on that as a sure-fire event.'

'Fine.' Without another word, Glory went back into his bedroom, grabbed up her travel bag and locked herself in the bathroom. Tears of hurt bewilderment stung her eyes as she took off the top and skirt, which she now thoroughly loathed. Something had happened, something serious that had upset him. But he had not the faintest intention of telling her what that something was or of sharing his feelings.

She put on jeans, a T-shirt and comfortable canvas shoes. She thought that he might have followed her into the bedroom to wait for her to emerge and then talk to her again but he had not. She wrote her address on the notepad by the phone. When she went downstairs again she found him standing by the superb marble fireplace in the gracious drawing-room, staring down with brooding intensity into the low-burning fire.

'I'm ready.'

'The car's outside. Don't go all female and huffy on me, *cara*,' Rafaello urged, shooting her a bleak glance from beneath his lush dark lashes. 'Tonight is just a case of bad timing—'

'Huffy? Why would I be huffy?' Glory demanded with stinging chagrin. 'All I'm hoping is that you use this weekend to think better of the idea of taking on an unwilling mistress!'

Rafaello focused dark golden eyes on her with sizzling effect. 'Unwilling? We'll find out in Corfu, won't we...?'

Three days later a Toyota Landcruiser whisked Glory away from the island airport.

She had flown out to Corfu cocooned in the incredible luxury of Rafaello's private jet and had been surprised to find that he was not on board. However, his aircrew had treated her like royalty and, although she had told herself that she was far too sensible to be impressed by rampant materialism, she had been impressed to death. His jet had been a far cry from the cramped and uncomfortable package holiday flight to Spain which she had endured with Sam a couple of years earlier. Served with a lunch that would have passed muster in a top-flight hotel, she had been offered a selection of recent films to watch and the latest copies of a dozen glossy magazines.

The Landcruiser branched off the busy main thoroughfare and eventually onto a rough road that climbed ever upward between groves of gnarled silver-green olive trees. They passed through quaint little hill villages on roads too narrow for two vehicles to pass at one and the same time. As they headed back down towards the coast on the other side of the island a series of tortuous bends and truly terrifying gradients slowed their journey even more. In all, it was an hour and a half and early evening before the car paused before a set of tall electronic gates that purred back for their entrance and drove up an avenue shaded by tall, graceful cypresses that cast long dark shadows like arrows.

The big villa was ultra-modern in design and pitched to take advantage of the sheltered seclusion of the lush green hillside and the fabulous sea views. A magnificent house in an even more magnificent setting, Glory conceded without much surprise as she climbed out of the car. But then, only the very best would satisfy a Grazzini. In the clear light in which every colour seemed sharper and brighter than it did back in England, the view of the brilliant blue Ionian Sea washing the golden strand only a hundred yards below her would have taken her breath away had not nervous tension already done that for her.

A middle-aged man in an old-fashioned steward's white jacket ushered her into a marble-tiled foyer and showed her into a superb galleried reception room that opened out onto a wooden viewing deck.

'Signor Grazzini will be with you soon, Miss Little,' the manservant informed her. 'Tea or coffee? Perhaps an aperitif before dinner?'

'Where *is* Signor Grazzini?' Glory enquired tautly, beginning to feel offensively like a parcel forever waiting to be picked up.

The older man looked uncomfortable.

'That's OK. I'll go and find him for myself.' Glory stalked back out to the hall, put her hands on her hips and yelled full volume, '*Rafaello?*'

Within fifteen seconds one of the doors off the spacious, airy hall jerked wide and Rafaello appeared. Clad in a lightweight pale cream suit, exquisitely tailored to his big, powerful frame, he looked nothing short of spectacular. He scanned her taut figure, taking in the patterned blue cotton shirt dress she wore and the plait in which she had restrained her hair.

'You wanted me here. I'm *here!*' Glory pointed out in the rushing silence, folding her arms in an effort to conceal the reality that she was trembling. For a crazy moment she had wanted to fling herself at him, and she had been shaken by that insane prompting.

'What a novel way to get attention…' a cut-glass English voice remarked.

Glory stiffened in dismay as a willowy brunette beauty with the exotic elegance of a supermodel strolled forward to stand by Rafaello's side. Resting one possessive hand on his sleeve and throwing him a covert glance in the age-old communication of one lover to another, she spelt out their intimacy in non-verbal ways that any woman would have understood. 'Really, I must try bellowing at the top of my voice when I next find that my host is not immediately available. So simple and effective.' The brunette completed her cutting little speech with saccharine-sweet scorn.

'Glory...this is Fiona Woodrow,' Rafaello told her with unblemished composure.

The brunette extended a languid hand. Her face having flamed and then paled to leave her as white as paper, Glory ignored that empty gesture. Hypocrisy was not one of her talents.

A door opened somewhere behind her. 'Jon...' Rafaello drawled in the calmest of tones. 'If you have the time, could you ensure that Glory gets a long cool drink?'

Jon Lyons escorted Glory out to the viewing deck. The sun was beginning to set over the beautiful bay below. The horizon was shot with the fiery splendour of crimson and gold. Hands clenched into fists of restraint by her side, Glory could not yet bring herself to look at the young blond man. Fiona Woodrow had made her feel small and stupid and crude in front of an audience but she blamed Rafaello entirely for that development.

The older man who had greeted her on her arrival appeared with a tray. A tall moisture-beaded glass and an artistic arrangement of tiny bite-sized appetisers were set down on the table beside which she stood.

'I would need a dip in the Arctic to cool me down,' Glory muttered finally, throwing a look of pained apology at Jon for her self-absorption. 'Who is Fiona?'

'Rafaello has been acquainted with Lady Fiona for a long time,' Jon Lyons responded after an awkward pause, his clean-cut features tense, his brown eyes veiled. 'I'm afraid that's as much as I know.'

Lady Fiona? A titled member of the British aristocracy. Glory bit down hard on her tongue and tasted the sweet tang of blood in her dry mouth. She folded her arms even tighter; indeed, felt as though that defensive barrier was crazily the only thing keeping her upright and together. Acquainted? What a delicate choice of word! The brunette had brandished the fact that her relationship with Rafaello was of the intimate variety. There was no avoiding the obvious: Rafaello had another woman. Furthermore, he had not even had the decency to get Fiona Woodrow out of the villa before Glory arrived. It was disgusting. It lacerated her pride, tore at her heart and terrified her all at one and the same time. Her emotions were on such a high, she could barely think straight.

'Does he have a lot of women he brings here? Is this like…the harem in the hills?' she demanded unsteadily.

Momentarily, Jon looked as though he might laugh. Then he met her anguished blue eyes, with a look of sympathy, he said reluctantly, 'The boss does get around. You can't really blame him—'

'Can't I?' Just then Glory needed no encouragement to heap all the sins of humanity on Rafaello's broad shoulders.

'Women go for him big-time.'

And why not? She had always wondered and now she knew for sure. Rafaello was a womaniser, spoilt for choice, spoilt by all the endless options and fresh faces available to a male with wealth, good looks and charm. Only where she herself was concerned the charm seemed to be in pretty short supply this time around.

But then, what else had she expected? He wasn't dating her, wasn't trying to please her. Caring concern and tact were not on his agenda. Suddenly she was facing unpleasant truths shorn of the hazy romantic images which had come from her own imagination alone. Of course Rafaello had not been on the flight out from England with her, of course he had not put himself out to come and meet her at the airport! All that he wanted from her was the use of her body. Casual, uncommitted sex. He had spelt that right out upfront. How had she managed to avoid facing that reality?

'Please don't be offended when I say that you don't fit the usual mould,' Jon Lyons confided in a wry undertone. 'You'll be history with Rafaello the minute he realises you're emotionally involved.'

'I'm not emotionally involved with him.' Wanting to boil Rafaello in oil and make him suffer the tortures of the damned while she watched and gloated was not emotional involvement on Glory's terms. In any case, she was *not* staying in Corfu to be a temporary distraction in any harem in the hills! Her brother, Sam, was safe. The theft charge had been withdrawn and her father had been reinstated. The crisis was over, the pressure on her already at an end. She had been able to confirm that on Saturday.

Sam had phoned her first thing that morning. She had been very surprised to learn that Rafaello had stayed talking with her father and Sam until well after midnight. What about the urgent business that had supposedly cropped up that same evening? Evidently, Rafaello had shown no apparent desire to cut his visit short. She had been even more surprised when Sam confided that Rafaello was, 'OK...in fact, quite a cool guy and very talkative.' To be frank, she had almost toppled over in shock when her kid brother had gone on to tell her that Rafaello had stated that in retrospect he felt that he might have rather overreacted to the whole situation.

Indeed, Rafaello had gone to extraordinary lengths to smooth matters over and Glory had been planning to thank him from the bottom of her heart for lying in his teeth. For, of course, he had been lying. She remembered how he had talked about having his home and his property 'violated' and had quite understood his feelings. But Rafaello's generous attitude of forgiveness had released her brother from his brooding depression and anxiety. She had not expected

Rafaello to recognise and understand just how vulnerable Sam could be.

That same evening Sam had phoned his friend, Joe, and, once reassured that confessing to stealing the snuff box would not result in his being charged in Sam's place, Joe had come over to own up and apologise to Rafaello face-to-face. Joe had taken the box on impulse, thinking it would make a nice present for his mother's birthday, but within half an hour of succumbing to temptation the teenager had panicked. He had hidden the tiny item in the Littles' fuel shed sooner than retain possession of it and had hoped that something so very small would not even be missed at the Park.

Emerging from the recollection of that enlightening phone call from her brother, Glory lifted the tall glass and let her parched mouth rejoice in the refreshing fruit drink. Sam might be all right now but it really was time that *she* grew up and let go of her old memories of Rafaello Grazzini. Fanciful girlish memories based on what? A mere six weeks with him? She would be much better recalling the manner in which he had humiliated her at the end of that brief relationship. He had been cruel, unnecessarily cruel. Just as he was being now in a far more careless way.

'If you want me to make that last flight, I should leave now,' she heard Jon say.

Turning her head to glance at him in confusion, Glory only then realised that Jon had been addressing Rafaello, who was poised several feet away. She set down her glass and tilted up her chin, shutting out those dark golden eyes which could exercise such frightening power over her. 'I might as well catch a lift with Jon if he's going to the airport. I'm not staying.'

The younger man dealt her a startled glance before he walked back indoors, discreetly removing himself from the proceedings.

'You're not going anywhere, *cara*,' Rafaello delivered with formidable cool.

'And how are you planning to stop me?' Glory enquired tightly, hanging on to her temper and her pain with fierce concentration, determined not to betray either or to give him the satisfaction of knowing how much he had hurt her by allowing her to meet Fiona Woodrow.

'With brute force if necessary.'

Glory opened her violet-blue eyes very wide to show how unimpressed she was by that threat. 'You wouldn't dare. I'd scream the place down.'

'Noise doesn't bother me. Being ripped off does, though.'

The tension sparked like invisible warning flares between them.

'That's right, be a real gentleman!' Glory snapped. 'Remind me about the callous agreement you forced on me—'

A winged black brow was elevated. '*Forced?* Didn't you trek all the way to Montague Park on Friday night dressed like a tart just for my benefit?'

'I was *not* dressed like a tart!' Glory hissed at him in outrage.

'Isn't that just like a woman?' Rafaello jerked loose his tie and cast it on the table. Her gaze widened slightly as, having undone his shirt collar, he proceeded to shrug with fluid grace out of the jacket of his suit. 'Parade the bait and then go into pious denial when the victim bites—'

'You are no woman's victim, Rafaello Grazzini!' Glory was infuriated by his line of argument. She had been desperate. She had believed that temptation was the only means of persuasion within her power. But whose fault was it that she had felt that she had to lower herself to that level? Who had spelt out those demeaning parameters? Who had made it brutally clear that in his opinion her looks were her only currency?

'That's right,' Rafaello confirmed, his smouldering dark

golden eyes holding hers full force. 'Glad you've divined that fact. Do you recall how you tried to play me for a fool five years ago? Do you also remember how that ended? I wasn't the one who fled in tears.'

'You bastard...' Glory framed in shaken outrage and pain. The very last thing she needed just then was the recollection of how devastated she had been at eighteen when he paraded her replacement, the merchant banker's daughter, in front of her.

Rafaello discarded his jacket on the table alongside his tie. 'I don't let anyone call me that,' he intoned in a lethal low-pitched drawl.

'Well, I just got away with it!' Glory slung in helpless triumph.

'You're not getting away with anything. It's all going on an account to be rendered with your name at the top. *Dio mio*, you think I'm a fool?'

'Look, I'm not going to waste time arguing with you.' That unsettling reference to an account being rendered had chilled Glory to the marrow. 'I'll get a lift with Jon back to the airport.'

'I said no.'

'Oh, wow...' Glory sounded out with syllabic thoroughness and all the scorn she could muster.

'I warned you.' Striding forward with an expression of calm intent stamped on his lean, strong face, Rafaello settled his hands to her waist and swept her off her feet.

In furious disbelief Glory swung back her arm and attempted to land a resounding slap on one hard male cheekbone but he ducked his head before it could connect. 'How dare you do that when I want to hit you?' she raged at him.

'If you try to hit me again I might just dump you in the pool to cool off,' Rafaello threatened with immovable cool as he hoisted her over his shoulder to prevent her flailing fists from doing any damage.

'I can't swim!' Glory gasped in horror.

'I'll get into the water with you, then, but dip you I will,' Rafaello swore, striding through the vast lounge into the hall.

'I'll call the police if you don't put me down!' Glory threatened in a rising screech.

'What with? Alien antennae?' Rafaello enquired.

Another voice entered the proceedings. 'Rafaello…' It was Jon Lyons' quiet voice and he cleared his throat with pronounced hesitancy before continuing. 'Do you really think you ought to be manhandling your guest like that?'

'Don't mess with what you don't understand,' Rafaello advised his executive assistant, galling amusement audible in his dark, deep drawl. 'Glory and I go way back in time—'

'No, we don't!' Glory braced her hands to his muscular back to raise her head, but she still couldn't see Jon Lyons because he was standing out of view. So enraged was she by the ridiculous figure she had to be cutting that she was surprised that flames weren't pouring from her mouth.

'Glory was four years old when we first met. She was at a Christmas party for the estate workers' children. She thumped a little boy who was chasing her with mistletoe. She was tiny but she attacked like a lion,' Rafaello recounted, making Glory blink in bewilderment as she listened. 'I hauled her off him before she got hurt and she was swinging her fists and screeching, "Let me at him!" She hasn't changed much.'

'You just made that whole story up.' Glory had no memory whatsoever of the episode he had described, although she had certainly attended those festive parties as a child. 'That never happened!'

Rafaello started to mount the stairs. 'I didn't notice you again until you were about thirteen, but don't get excited at that news. It wasn't you who first attracted my attention. It was the incessant car horns being sounded by admiring male drivers while you stood at the bus stop in the morning and I was driving past. Then, after you moved into the gardener's cottage, I used to see you lurking in the rhododendrons beside the main drive, slapping on the paint before you could face the school bus.'

Glory was so stunned by that second even lengthier speech, her luscious mouth fell inelegantly wide.

'I can see I was out of line interfering...' From the hall below, Jon Lyons punctuated that retreat with a rueful laugh. 'When you said *way back* you weren't joking, Rafaello. It sounds like you two practically grew up together. I'll see you next week.'

As the front door thudded shut downstairs and silence enclosed them again Glory balled both hands into furious fists and struck at Rafaello's back again. 'What were you doing sneaking through the bushes when I was putting on my lip gloss?' she demanded for want of anything better to attack with at that moment.

'When I was back from university I used to go out running in the morning. You were such a vain little creature. You used to sit endlessly combing your hair like a mermaid on a rock.'

'You *spied* on me!' Glory accused shakily. 'I was not being vain!'

'I avoided the main drive after I saw you there a couple of times. Spying on little schoolgirls wasn't my style then or now.'

'Mum wouldn't let me style my hair or use make-up like my friends did, and I used to do myself up a bit before I went for the bus,' she protested with fierce defensiveness. 'I was *not* vain. Haven't you ever heard of peer pressure? Put me down, Rafaello!'

Rafaello lowered her to the carpet in a lovely bedroom. French windows stood wide on a balcony on the far side of the room. The silk curtains were fluttering in the gentle breeze. For an instant the unusual bed engaged her attention. The tall headboard had an ornate carved frame and what appeared to be tiny pictures with silver surrounds set into the polished surface. Frowning over her momentary distraction, Glory headed straight back towards the door through which she had been carried. 'You can stop acting like a caveman right now.'

Rafaello was lounging back against the door with folded arms. His white shirt open at his strong brown throat, his devastatingly dark and handsome face set with intent, he looked back at her with challenging golden eyes. 'So tell me, what made you *suddenly* decide to go home again?'

Glory stiffened and paled. 'If you think I'm willing to be another in the long line of your tarts, you'd better think again!' she launched back grittily.

'Welcome to the fold, *bella mia*.' Rafaello's delivery was as smooth as silk.

CHAPTER FIVE

'DID I just hear you say what I thought I heard you say?' Glory demanded with stark incredulity.

'I was hoping provocation would get you to the crux of the matter.' Rafaello's glinting, lustrous dark gaze rested on her. 'Fiona's parents own a villa just along the coast. She's a regular visitor and I wasn't expecting her. You're throwing a tantrum because Fiona was here when you arrived and she embarrassed you…or you embarrassed yourself.'

Glory's lovely face flamed as if he had lit a bonfire inside her. So much had passed between them in the last few minutes that she did not know where to begin in arguing or defending herself. 'I don't throw tantrums like some spoilt brat demanding attention. But, whether you like it or not, I do have standards—'

'But offer you enough cash and you drop them,' Rafaello slotted in with lethal timing.

'Oh…so we're back to the cheque I accepted when I was eighteen, are we?' Although Glory felt severely undermined by his referring to that episode again, she squared her slight shoulders and tossed her honey-blonde head high. 'I suppose it's time that I told you the truth about that. I let Dad have that money because he needed it. Your father forced me to leave my home.'

'And how did Benito do that?' Rafaello enquired with extreme dryness and the kind of outrageous aura of unspoken disbelief that made her want to scream and force him to listen to her with an open mind.

'For goodness' sake, Dad was drinking at the time. I know you never mentioned it but you must've known about

75

his alcohol problem,' Glory asserted in a strained undertone. 'Your father threatened to sack him unless I moved away and broke off all contact with you. Dad would never have stopped drinking if he'd lost his job and his home as well.'

Silence had fallen. Rafaello was very still, his fabulous bone-structure defined by hard tension. But his ice-cool dark eyes were now bleak and unimpressed. 'How very distasteful it would be if you were telling the truth. But I have *very* good cause to know that Benito would never have sacked your father or left him and your brother homeless,' he asserted with harsh conviction. 'You're talking about blackmail. You're lying in your teeth.'

Although Glory had known that Rafaello would not easily credit her story, it was none the less a blow when he rejected her version of events with such immediacy. Furthermore she neither understood nor believed his assurance that Benito Grazzini would *never* have sacked her father and put him out of the cottage. After all, any employer would eventually sack a drunken worker and would feel little need to defend their action. Why would Rafaello's father have felt any different? Compassion only went so far.

'Why try to wrap up what really happened?' Rafaello was now studying her with derision curling his wide, sensual mouth. 'You got the offer to be a model and you couldn't wait to grab at what you believed was your chance for fame and fortune. You had already decided to leave home, so you simply accepted the financial bribe my father offered you.'

So that was how he had reasoned it all out to satisfy himself as to her guilt and greed. It was a tidy reading of past events but it was *not* what had happened. Then she had been foolish to hope that Rafaello would even consider accepting her word over his father's.

Letting his allegations lie unchallenged, for she saw no

good reason to continue a losing battle, Glory said flatly, 'I meant what I said downstairs…I'm leaving. If you're so keen to have a mistress, why don't you ask Lady Fiona? She seemed more than willing!'

'For no good reason that my brain can comprehend, I want you much more.' Rafaello strolled away from the door at a leisurely pace.

'I'm not getting mixed up with a man who is carrying on with other women—'

'As far as I can see, my bed's empty… Fiona and I have a history, but that's not something I intend to discuss with you, *cara*.' Rafaello came to a halt only inches away from her and reached for the long plait curling over her shoulder with a calm hand.

'What are you doing?' Glory spat, feeling threatened by his proximity.

'I like the mermaid hair loose.'

'Do you think I care what you like?'

'I believe you can learn if I give you lessons in easy stages, *bella mia*.'

She encountered sizzling dark golden eyes and her breath snarled up in her throat. His fingers were busy unravelling her hair. All she had to do to bring an end to that liberty was put some distance between them, but she stayed where she was. 'I'm no good at learning what I don't want to learn.' Glory recognized the edge of desperation in her own voice. 'Let me go home. This is not going to work, Rafaello—'

'Let me be the judge of that—'

'But you *said* you wanted an experienced lover,' Glory reminded him in a last-ditch attempt to persuade him that she was not the kind of woman he really wanted. 'I'm an amateur—'

'Well, I didn't want a professional,' Rafaello told her, quick as a flash with the repartee.

Her colour heightened. 'I'm a virgin.'

The lean fingers engaged in slowly disentangling her hair stilled. 'That's not even funny.'

She gritted her teeth. 'I wasn't trying to be—'

Rafaello cupped her elbows to hold her still in front of him. He gazed down at her with wondering eyes. 'If you were Pinocchio, your nose would reach as far as the front door. A virgin? *You?* Even five years back, I wasn't entirely convinced by the purity pleas but I gave you the benefit of the doubt. I could hardly argue.'

Glory breathed very deep. 'What makes you so sure that I'm not?'

'You're too sexy,' Rafaello responded without hesitation. 'You move, you walk and you talk like a woman who knows her own body—'

'I've lived inside it a long time—'

'Virgins are a rarefied species. I've never met one your age—'

'You ask every woman you meet, do you?' Glory snapped, out of all patience and increasingly offended and angry rather than embarrassed. As she pulled her arms free Rafaello settled his lean, strong hands onto her rigid shoulders instead. 'Well, it's about time you woke up to the fact that there are quite a few women who don't believe in putting sex on a level with having a takeaway—'

'I don't eat takeaways either. I am irredeemably attached to the gastronomic delights provided by my French chef. Tell me, are you trying to make me feel guilty about our arrangement? Is that why you're suddenly telling whoppers the size of Jonah's whale?' Rafaello enquired with sardonic bite. 'If I thought you were a virgin I'd run like hell. But I know you can't be. I know it the way I know the earth is round.'

That seemed fairly conclusive. But he had hurt her. It hurt her even more to realise that he had even doubted her innocence five years earlier. He was such a cynic, but more than anything else he was revealing that he had always seen her just as other men saw her: in the most demeaning light. As a blonde bombshell, a sure thing, not too bright and bound to be promiscuous. But at least he had explained Fiona Woodrow's presence to her satisfaction, hadn't he?

Glory worried at her full lower lip with her teeth and looked up at him in sudden Stark appeal. 'I just don't *want* to be your mistress—'

'You really ought to stop me taking your dress off, then. I warn you, once I catch a glimpse of delectable bare skin I will use every trick in the book to get you horizontal.'

So intent on her troubled thoughts had Glory been that she hadn't noticed that he had unzipped her dress. Now she gazed down in frank confusion as he eased the garment slowly from her shoulders and down over her slender arms, exposing the pouting swell of breasts cupped in white lace. 'Rafaello, n-no...'

'I can put my hand on my heart right now and admit that nothing has ever turned me on harder and faster than your gorgeous breasts,' Rafaello confessed with earthy male appreciation.

Conscious of him with every fibre of her being, Glory trembled. Unprompted, the dress drifted down over her hands and dropped to her feet. She recognized the burning hunger in his intent gaze and the most terrible physical weakness flooded her. All natural modesty was overborne by the realisation that he was admiring her, appreciating her. The wanton side of her nature adored that and thrilled to the reassurance that he liked what he was seeing. Then it was what she had always secretly sought from him. She had *always* wanted Rafaello to be her first lover, her last lover, her forever lover. Temptation was pulling at her hard. Why shouldn't she pretend that something other than the cold arrangement he had offered had brought them together again? Hadn't she spent five years fruitlessly seeking a male who could make her feel like Rafaello had once made her feel?

Rafaello gathered her up into his strong arms and carried her over to the huge bed. 'I have been waiting a very long time to do this.'

As he threw back the bedspread and settled her down on the crisp white linen sheet Glory whispered, 'Honestly?'

He plucked off her shoes and straightened with easy grace to stare down at her. '*Per amor di Dio*, how could you doubt that?'

Glory's look collided with his stunning golden gaze and her heart started to pound. Yet, lying down, she felt so much more self-conscious than she had standing. Her bra and panties might cover a great deal more of her than most beachwear but never had she been more aware of her own body and never had she felt less clothed.

'You're the only woman who has ever denied me. A clever move, that...' Rafaello was unbuttoning his shirt, a slanting smile on his beautifully shaped mouth. 'Perhaps that's why I want you so much, *bella mia*.'

Hurt tinged her growing apprehension. 'It wasn't a move. I wasn't trying to be clever—'

'Weren't you?' He cast off his shirt. 'It doesn't matter now.'

But it mattered to her that he should hold such an unrelentingly low opinion of her. Yet she could not retain that level of concentration, not when she was seeing Rafaello shorn of his shirt for the first time. Five years ago he had invited her to join him for a swim in the indoor pool up at the Park but she had made excuses not only because she couldn't swim but also because she had feared that folk would say that Glory Little was *really* getting above herself. She had endured enough cracks about 'mixing with the toffs', had soon learned that people were, at the very least, uncomfortable watching the gardener's daughter dating Benito Grazzini's son and heir. The very last thing she would have risked was being seen swanning round the Grazzinis' luxurious pool complex.

Now her mouth went dry as she focused on the hard, muscular planes of Rafaello's chest and the taut flatness of his abdomen. He was absolutely gorgeous, just as she had known he would be. His bronzed skin, rippling muscles and the haze of crisp black curls sprinkling his pectorals were overpoweringly male and sexy. She discovered that she could not take her attention from him for a moment lest she miss the chance to admire a different angle of view. Her face burned with colour at that acknowledgement. Pulling herself up against the pillows, she more covertly scanned his narrow hips and long, powerful thighs as he shed his well-cut trousers.

'I hope you're planning to do the same for me,' Rafaello drawled softly.

'Sorry?'

Rafaello, clad solely in a pair of black silk boxer shorts, sent her a wolfish look of all-male amusement. 'I can feel your eyes devouring me like fire.'

Glory reddened to the roots of her hair and ducked behind it, belatedly grateful that he had undone her plait and given her that amount of cover. 'Obviously you'd like to think so—'

'Lust can recognise lust,' Rafaello assured her, stripping off his last garment with a level of cool she could not credit, for certainly she could not mirror his self-possession.

There he was, totally revealed, and she was stunned. Naturally she had been a bit curious as to what a man looked like when... But wondering had not kept her awake at night. Indeed, in the past, registering that a man was physically aroused by her had always made her feel instinctively disgusted, only noteably that had *not* been her reaction to Rafaello. However, now seeing him in that naked state truly shook her, for she had never dreamt that he would be quite so intimidating.

'We're not going to fit.' Glory mumbled in a strangled voice, and then so appalled was she that panic had pro-

voked her to say such a thing and out loud, she shut her
eyes tight and cringed for herself in embarrassment.

'Is that a compliment, *bella mia*?' She could hear the
smile in his dark accented drawl, the satisfaction. He was
irrepressible, she thought in furious mortification.

'Even your little shell-like ears are turning scarlet,'
Rafaello noted with amusement.

'No, they're not!' Glory gasped, whipping up her hands
to touch the offending parts and discovering that they did
indeed feel rather warm and hurriedly pulling her hair over
them in concealment.

As the mattress gave slightly beneath her she realised
she had company on the bed and her eyes flew wide. She
connected head-on with eyes as golden as dazzling sunlight, all the more accentuated by the effect of his spiky
black lashes and the bronzed hue of his staggeringly attractive lean, dark face. It was like jamming her finger in
an electric current. His sheer sizzling appeal bereaved her
of breath and made her heart thump like a demented road
drill.

'Come here…' Rafaello urged huskily, lean hands closing on her forearms to tug her closer.

From that first moment, he gave no quarter. He caught
her mouth under his and plundered her soft pink lips with
molten hunger. She shivered in sensual shock, her breath
rasping in her throat and turning into ragged little gasps as
he continued that marauding assault at full pitch. His
tongue danced and mated with hers and then darted deep
with a rhythmic eroticism that she was defenceless against.
He had once taught her that just kissing could be incredibly
exciting, and his technique reduced her to the level of absolute compliance.

Rafaello released her swollen mouth and surveyed her
passion-glazed face with hotly appreciative eyes. 'We're
supposed to be seated downstairs enjoying a long and leisurely meal by candlelight—'

'I couldn't eat!' Glory exclaimed in dismay as if he was threatening her with that possibility.

'Later…' Rafaello seemed to taste the word as if he was savouring the far more entertaining alternatives currently available to him.

Only brute force could have dragged Glory from him at that moment. As she stared up into his mesmeric bright eyes he hooked an expert finger in the front fastening on her bra and the cups parted, releasing her full breasts into his reverent hands. Her throat closed over on the almost painful surge of sensation that assailed her as he touched her there for the first time without clothing to dull her own response. All Rafaello had to do was brush his thumbs over the throbbing pink peaks of her nipples and she was lost beyond redemption. She loosed a moan she could not restrain and her face burned hot with embarrassment because he was watching her.

'You denied us even this much five years ago,' Rafaello reminded her in raw-edged reproof.

As he rubbed the tender buds straining for his attention she was trembling beneath the rising strength of her own response. Had she had breath she could have told him that, with hindsight, her caution then had been very wise. Even now, she did not have the control to deny herself and would have had considerably less when she loved him. No matter how tough it had been to lose him, she knew it would have been ten times tougher and more demeaning had he succeeded in seducing her into bed with him.

'I'm going to drive you crazy with desire, *cara*.' It was both threat and promise combined.

'You already got there,' Glory framed unevenly, torn between exhilaration at her own intoxication and fear at the effect he was having on her.

Rafaello tipped her back and rearranged her to his satisfaction, fanning out her honey-blonde hair over the pillows when it caught beneath her shoulder. 'I'm only beginning…'

He tugged up her knees and lifted her to extract her from her panties in one smooth movement. And the very smoothness with which he did that jolted her into wondering how many other women it must have taken to develop that amount of expertise. That hurt enough to make her think, but then that arrogant dark head lowered. He captured a rosy nub between his lips and proceeded to torment her sensitive flesh without conscience. Before very long the stroke of his wicked tongue and the glide of his even white teeth had reduced her to a level where concentration was an impossible challenge.

'I already knew you had a perfect body,' Rafaello groaned, scanning her hectically flushed face with earthy male approval. 'But I had no idea that you might also be every man's fantasy of the perfect lover, *bella mia*.'

Challenged to speak as well as respond, Glory blinked up at him, feeling she must have misheard him. 'A… fantasy?'

'You heat up fast.' Rafaello extended, running an appreciative hand down over a slender thigh and employing a judicious knee to deftly separate it from its partner.

Glory tensed, not so sure a fast heat-up rate was a compliment to be cherished. Suddenly she was feeling very vulnerable, apprehensively aware of the boldness of his arousal as he shifted against her hip, wondering if there was even the remotest hope of waves beating on distant sunny seashores in store for her. Or whether something like the one or two more disturbing experiences she had heard other women share with blunt amusement might be her lot instead.

'If you hurt me, I'm not doing this again,' she warned him tautly.

'*Accidenti?*' Rafaello dealt her a startled appraisal. '*Hurt* you? I'm not going to hurt you. I've never hurt a woman in my life!'

Grateful for that reassurance, Glory put up no objection to the sensually tender kiss he seemed to use to soothe her with action as much as words. Indeed, within a very short space of time she forgot her apprehension. True, she tensed when he let his fingers roam through the tangle of blonde curls at the apex of her slender thighs, but then he reached a place so impossibly sensitive to his skilful attentions that thinking about what came next was quite beyond her. She had never dreamt that she was capable of feeling what she felt then. Sunk into mindless pleasure and writhing uncontrollably with a hunger that felt wicked, greedy and utterly devouring, she ached and burned to a height of excitement that felt unbearable.

When she could no longer stand that gnawing ache for satisfaction Rafaello seemed miraculously to understand. But, just as he was hauling her under him with a degree of wild, needy impatience that she found even more exciting in the mood that she was in, he paused and stretched away from her to yank open the drawer in the bedside cabinet.

Entirely in the grip of her shameless, feverish hunger, Glory listened to him mutter a fierce imprecation in Italian and regarded him with blank eyes.

'Are you OK?' Rafaello ground out, staring down at her with what looked remarkably like a prayer in his gorgeous eyes.

He was asking her permission, she thought, which, considering that he was trembling with eagerness against her, seemed very considerate and sweet.

She raised her hand and let her fingertips trail in a caress beneath the taut line of his shapely mouth. 'Yes...of course.'

With an air of intense relief Rafaello claimed another passionate kiss and slid his hands beneath her hips to tip her back. She felt the hot, urgent probe of his shaft against her most tender flesh and she was so driven by the tormenting ache for fulfilment he had roused in her, she urged him on in a movement as old as time itself by rising up to him and wrapping herself round him. He answered that invitation with a driving thrust. For the first instant, she was shocked by the sensation of invasion, and, for the second, overwhelmed by responsive pleasure to that incredible intimacy. Then came a sharp, stabbing pain that wrenched her from her sensual spell with a vengeance, and she cried out.

Rafaello stilled and gazed down at her with an expression of shattered disbelief. 'You *can't* be...' he whispered half under his breath.

There was no mistaking the level of his shock at the discovery that she had not been lying about the precise extent of her experience. Stunned golden eyes gazed down into hers.

Something perilously akin to smugness eased the dying remnants of physical discomfort Glory was suffering. She liked the idea that she had shattered his image of her and proven it to be false.

'I'll stop...' Rafaello gritted, taking her aback with that decision in turn.

Glory closed both arms round him, let her fingers delve through the thick silk of his black hair, scanning the lean, strong features so close to her own. 'Might as well finish,' she mumbled, hot-faced, telling herself that she didn't want him thinking she was a tease by calling a halt at what could not be said to be a good moment for him.

'*Si...bella mia,*' he muttered with a flattering amount of appreciation. '*Per meraviglia...*stopping now would kill me!'

Generosity felt very good at that point. While she was resigning herself to enduring the rest of it for his sake while striving to explain to herself why she should feel so self-sacrificing all of a sudden, Rafaello took her even more by

surprise. He surged into her with an immense gentleness
that she found incredibly touching and then, to her astonishment, even more enjoyable. Her eyes opened very wide.

'I'll make it good,' Rafaello swore with roughened tenderness.

Her heart started accelerating to a hammer-beat again
and everything she had been feeling before that brief instant
of pain returned to her tenfold. Suddenly she was with him
again, losing the power of thought and then control, arching
up to match his fluid thrusts, discovering a pagan rhythm
all of her own. Her breath coming in shallow pants, she
gave herself up to the powerful excitement building higher
and higher within her. He drove her, gasping, to a dizzy
peak and nothing could have surpassed the sheer wondrous
sensation that gripped her writhing body with an ecstasy of
pleasure.

Glory drifted back to the land of the living to find herself
still plastered as close to Rafaello as an extra layer of skin.
Finding no fault whatsoever with that discovery, she snug-
gled even closer and could not control the dreamy smile
stretching her mouth. Paradise was being in his arms, she
decided, breathing in the hot, damp, sexy scent of him as
if he was a drug she needed to survive. She felt amazingly
tender and affectionate towards him and only just resisted
an urge to smother him in loving kisses.

Rafaello tensed. 'Quit snuggling,' he told her drily.

Glory froze as if the roof had come down on top of her.
Before she could even react to that apparent rejection that
just seized her up with pain, Rafaello rolled her flat onto
her back against the pillows and leant over her. He brushed
her tumbled honey-blonde hair back from her brow,
dropped an unexpected kiss on her reddened mouth and
smiled down at her.

It was that glorious smile that finally convinced her that
she had misread his signals. When he had urged her to quit
he had been teasing, and her heart went crazy when she

recognised the easy humour curving the relaxed line of his sculpted mouth. 'You have really shocked me,' he confided huskily.

Glory kept on smiling. All was right within her immediate world. She was brimming full of happiness purely because he was happy. By no means did he look dissatisfied by his recent discovery that she was not the skilful partner he had expected. And in no way was she dissatisfied with him.

'I've got no excuse. I can't defend myself. I *should* have listened to you, *bella mia*,' Rafaello conceded with an amount of regretful humility she would never have believed a male of his unquenchable assurance could display.

'Yes, you should've,' Glory agreed, but she was quick to snake her arms round him again lest he think she was withholding forgiveness.

'I'm just amazed,' Rafaello admitted, surveying her with frowning fascination. 'You've been knee-deep in predatory men all these years and you didn't succumb to one of them. Yet you're not a cold woman.'

'You're more persuasive than the rest,' Glory confided shyly.

'Evidently...' Rafaello rolled over and sat up. 'You've just blown a great big hole in my image of you as calculating.'

'I guess...' Glory was now feeling so buoyant she was vaguely surprised that she wasn't floating round the ceiling. Flipping onto her side, she surveyed him. Dear heaven, just looking at him made her feel dreamy and silly. She wanted to ease back into physical contact with him but was afraid of seeming too clingy. She wanted to hug him again. She wanted to tell him he was wonderful...she wanted to tell him she loved him. Odd how she had wanted to tell him that before she had even admitted it to herself, she acknowledged in a daze. It was pretty naff, her still being so keen on him after five years apart, she reflected ruefully. It didn't say much for her ability to move on, did it? But then, it was not something she planned to share with him.

'Although I confess to being very grateful that you were sufficiently calculating to accept that we were going to end up in bed sooner rather than later,' Rafaello was saying while he toyed with a straying blonde strand of her wildly tousled mane of hair.

Glory's brow furrowed. She wondered if she had missed a line of explanation somewhere. 'Sorry…what do you mean?'

Rafaello released a rueful sigh and tugged at her hair as to reprove her for her evident lack of concentration. 'When I realised that the only contraception I had was in another room I was very relieved to discover that you were better organised than I was, *cara*.'

Glory was now very still and when her voice emerged it was rather strained. 'Better organised?'

'On my last stay here, this room was being decorated and I used the one next door,' he explained.

Glory remembered his opening the drawer in the bedside cabinet. Having only briefly wondered what he was looking for, she now felt unbelievably stupid. Rafaello had been reaching for protection.

'A virgin who takes care of contraception in advance is a very sensible woman.'

To Glory, that statement seemed to hang there in the air between them like a giant rock about to fall on her. Her opinion of her own common sense dive-bombed. 'But…but I didn't take care of contraception,' she admitted in a very small voice.

'Run that by me again,' Rafaello breathed, abandoning all play with her hair, his Italian accent screaming at her the way it always did when he was very tense.

'I'm not taking any precautions or using anything,' Glory clarified shakily.

Rafaello's hard jawline clenched. Narrowed dark eyes

scanned her anxious upturned face and an expression of
incredulous fury slowly fired his gaze. In a sudden movement that made her flinch, he sprang out of the bed. 'But
I *asked* you if it was OK to make love to you!'

A silence, fragile as a sheet of glass about to smash,
stretched.

Her heart sinking, Glory gulped. 'When I said yes, I
thought you meant that question literally...I didn't know
you were asking whether or not it might be s-safe,' she
stammered, ready to curl up and die as she realised how
foolish she had been. 'I didn't think—'

'You didn't think. So you're trying to say that it was
only a simple misunderstanding?' Rafaello ground out, glittering dark golden eyes smouldering with furious condemnation, his accent thick as molasses. 'Do you honestly think
I'll believe anything that unlikely?'

'What else could it have been but a misunderstanding?'
Glory was sincerely taken aback by his attitude.

'How about a textbook case of entrapment?' Rafaello
shot at her with lethal contempt, his hard cheekbones prom-
inent beneath his bronzed skin, accentuating his ferocious
tension.

'Entrapment?' she repeated without comprehension.

'I really fell for it, didn't I?' Rafaello raked at her
fiercely. 'And, knowing my luck where you're concerned,
you'll probably fall pregnant—'

'I hope not...' It was a stricken whisper.

Shattered by his suspicions, Glory was frozen to the bed.
How could he think that she would deliberately run the risk
of unprotected sex? How could he believe that she would
welcome an unplanned pregnancy? The mere prospect of
such a development terrified Glory. She had an instant vision of unwed motherhood combined with horrendous pov-
erty. One or two of her schoolfriends had taken that route
within a couple of years of leaving school and had lived to
regret the choice.

'Do you really? If I've knocked you up I'll be keeping you and the kid for the next twenty years at least!' Rafaello informed her in outraged conclusion. 'That's a bloody high price to pay for your precious virginity. I need a shower!'

As he strode into the connecting bathroom and the door slammed shut Glory felt gutted. Her happiness had been so short-lived that it now seemed like an illusion she had dreamt up. How could he imagine that she would sink that low? Was there no end to his distrust? What sort of an idiot had she been to think that she could so easily change his opinion of her? And wasn't she now getting exactly what she deserved for her foolishness?

Nothing was ever going to change. He was very rich. She was poor. There was no equality and there never would be. Without the equality, maybe respect and trust could not exist, she reasoned wretchedly. She was Glory Little, the gardener's daughter, the gypsy's daughter, the factory worker. He was Rafaello Grazzini, an extremely successful businessman and famed for his entrepreneurial skills.

He was *hurting* her again. How could she be letting him do that to her a second time? Didn't she ever learn? She had agreed to be his mistress. He had said he only wanted sex. She had given him what he wanted. End of story. What on earth had she been doing, clinging to him? *A textbook case of entrapment?* Glory shuddered, nausea stirring in her sensitive stomach. As if she was some greedy, scheming little tramp he had picked up off a street corner!

She threw herself off the bed and viewed the tangled bed-sheets with shamefaced discomfiture. Well, retribution had come even faster than she had warned. 'If you don't value yourself, no man will,' her mother had once told her harshly. So what had she expected to achieve when she had *sold* herself? Choking tears of regret clogging her aching throat, Glory knew she needed to get a grip on herself before she risked facing Rafaello again. But her dress was nowhere to be seen. Just as she was wondering if her dress lay beneath the bedspread heaped on the carpet, she heard the shower switch off and panic filled her.

As her case was still downstairs, she raced over to the sleek built-in units that covered one wall and yanked open a door. Seeing a row of shirts hanging, she trailed one off a hanger and dug her arms into it at frantic speed. Within ten seconds she was out of the bedroom and hurrying down the stairs. Catching a glimpse of Rafaello's manservant clearing a table in one of the ground-floor rooms, she realised that the only true sanctuary available was the outdoors. As she sped out of the front door, emerging into the bright path of the outside lights, she found herself in the very teeth of a surprisingly strong wind. But she hesitated only a moment before she fled down the path to the beach and into the cover of the tamarisk trees ringing the cove.

CHAPTER SIX

GLORY could not credit that she had come out to a fabulous, scenic Greek island in the month of June only to find herself fighting to walk through a howling gale with sand blowing in her face.

The sea was foaming like a cauldron, mirroring the seething tempest of emotion inside her. Rafaello despised her. He truly did. She had to accept that but she didn't want to accept that, couldn't *bear* to accept that, she discovered. All the messy feelings she had buried five years earlier were escaping their bonds. Taking shelter beneath an overhanging rock in the massive outcrop near the end of the beach, she sat down, closing out the angry surge of the surf. With those painful emotions came the memories...

Glory had left school at sixteen. She had wanted to stay on but her father had asserted that no Little had ever been academic, and she had found work as an office junior at the local auctioneers. By the time she reached eighteen, sightings of Rafaello had become rare events. After all, the Grazzinis had divided their time between their Italian and English homes and, having completed his business degree, Rafaello had bought a London apartment and only visited Montague Park occasionally.

Glory had taken a long time to come to terms with their first humiliating encounter when she was sixteen and the horror of having been delivered home to her furious parents like a juvenile delinquent. When, afterwards, Rafaello would drive past Glory and award her a nod or smile of recognition, she would barely raise her head in acknowledgement. Yet, in spite of the lack of encouragement, one

week after her eighteenth birthday Rafaello had raked his
Ferrari to a halt in the drive and offered her a lift.

'Chance would be a fine thing,' Glory had told him
through the window he lowered, straining every sinew to
play it cool while striving not to overdo it.

'How would you like to go out to dinner tonight?'

She had got into his passenger seat almost before he
finished speaking.

'That was the magic combination, was it?' Rafaello had
murmured with a slanting smile that turned her all-too-
vulnerable heart upside-down and left her dizzy.

'Maybe I'm just hungry.' The truth would have been that
she had *never* been invited out for a meal. The males she
met invited her to bars, clubs, sports fixtures and the cin-
ema.

For the following six weeks Glory had walked on air and
her feet hadn't touched the ground once. True, mixing with
his friends had sometimes been a strain. She had discovered
entire conversational topics that had previously been un-
known to her. Winter skiing, opera, ballet, yachting and the
total agony of not being able to locate the latest must-have
designer handbag. While warning her that only grief could
be coming in her direction, her own friends had pooled their
clothes and loaned her outfits to wear. Dating Rafaello had
been something of a community effort.

The talent scout who had sighted her out at a club one
evening had tried to get her to sign up with a modelling
agency in the north. She had felt terribly flattered but
Rafaello had squashed any dreams she might have cherished on that score at source.

'You're too small to be a fashion model. The guy can't
be legit. Alternatively, you could find yourself fronting a
knitting pattern or some such thing.'

Which Glory had quite understood roughly translated
into the news that *he* did not want her chasing after a modelling career a few hundred miles away. Since the only

thing in her life she truly cared about at that time was *him*, she had thought no more about that offer. Soon after that Rafaello had persuaded her to let him give her a tour of Montague Park, but before they had even completed the circuit of the ground floor his father had interrupted them. Glory had immediately recognised that Benito Grazzini, though he made every effort to hide the fact, was very much shocked to discover that his son was dating his gardener's daughter.

'He doesn't like me seeing you,' she had said to Rafaello afterwards.

'He was just surprised. That's all. You're too sensitive,' Rafaello had told her.

But that same week Benito Grazzini had called at the cottage on Glory's afternoon off. Even worse, that same day her own father was upstairs sleeping off his drinking excesses, rather than out working as he should have been. Ironically, Benito Grazzini had looked awful, his eyes sunk in his head as if he hadn't slept for days and his greyish pallor no more healthy. But he had wasted no time in spelling out his terms.

As soon as he had told her that her father would be sacked if she did not do as he asked, she had known she had no choice. If she appealed to Rafaello for support she would only be making trouble which would rebound on her family. Rafaello was close to his father but she had only been dating him for a paltry six weeks, and, while she might be in love with him, he had made no such claims. Sobered up, Archie Little had fully supported his daughter's decision to surrender and leave home.

Glory had decided that the easiest way out of her predicament would be to tell Rafaello that she was accepting the modelling offer. At the time, Rafaello had been only weeks off spending four months setting up a branch office in Rome and she had already been afraid that that separation would end his interest in her. However, she *had* naïvely believed that they could part as friends.

The following afternoon that she spent with Rafaello had been one long, agonising torment for her to endure until she worked up the courage to tell him that she was going away as well.

'Let me get this straight...*you* are dumping *me*?' Rafaello had interrupted with a stunned look stamped on his darkly handsome features.

'No, it's not like that. It's just that I'm leaving and you're going to be abroad most of the time...I can't imagine when we'd see each other, so isn't a clean break better?'

'It's no big deal,' Rafaello had confirmed while he smiled steadily at her.

Then she had become the author of her own humiliation. It had already been arranged that they would join his friends for dinner that evening at an exclusive local restaurant. 'Can we still go ahead with tonight?' Glory had begged, desperate to spend every last possible moment with him.

'Why not?'

He had called her an hour before he was due to pick her up to inform her that he would be late and that he would meet her there instead. He had even sent a taxi for her and she had had not a clue what was waiting for her on her arrival. She could still remember that long, slow walk across the restaurant and her own stumbling, demeaning retreat from the sight of Rafaello kissing the very lovely redhead before he pulled away again.

As if it was a moment trapped in time she recalled how he had looked across the table at her with callous cool as though he didn't recognise her, as though she was nothing, nobody. It had felt as though everyone in the room was staring at her and laughing, and his friends had certainly been entertained by the scene of her downfall.

Rafaello hadn't changed, Glory reflected wretchedly as

her mind returned to the more pressing problems of the present. He always assumed the worst and he attacked without hesitation. Would he have been so quick to accuse a woman who came from his own privileged background? Of course not. But assuming that Glory could only be on the make came very naturally to him. She shivered, only then registering that the sea spray lashing off the rocks had soaked her to the skin.

'Glory!'

Hearing that shout, she tensed and saw Rafaello running through the surf towards the rocks. His pale shirt and trousers glimmered in the moonlight. Evidently he had come out in as much of a hurry as she had, for he was barefoot. The wind whipped his shirt back from his bronzed, muscular chest.

'*Glory!*' He sounded frantic and she felt childish hiding from him.

Slowly and stiffly, because her chilled limbs were numb, she emerged from her shelter. For a split-second, Rafaello stilled when he saw her and then he powered over to her at even greater speed. He caught her to him. 'When I couldn't find you I thought you had drowned,' he launched down at her in raw condemnation. 'Don't you ever do this to me again!'

Glory looked up at him in astonishment. Drowned? His lean, strong hands were biting into her slight shoulders. That he had been genuinely scared that something might have happened to her was etched into the fierce lines of his hard-boned features and the intensity with which he was staring down at her. 'Oh, you'd have managed to come to terms with me drowning,' Glory heard herself say none the less. 'After all, if I was pregnant my death would be a very cost-effective solution.'

'*Per amor di Dio*…how can you even say such a thing?' Rafaello dealt her a hard look of censure, dark, deep-set eyes scanning her with angry disbelief. 'What sort of a bastard do you think I am?'

'You said it,' Glory told him unsteadily, and she shivered.

'You're cold as ice…and you're wet.' Rafaello banded a strong arm to her spine and urged her back along the beach. 'The sirocco wind can kick up a storm in the space of minutes. If you had stumbled into the water at this end of the strand there's a steep drop just feet out. You can't swim. Naturally, I was worried.'

Unmoved, cold and weary, Glory said nothing. Typical that he should assume she was too stupid to stay out of a roaring sea, she thought grimly. At the foot of the sloping path he bent and scooped her up into his arms. 'You're exhausted,' he grated. 'Once you've had a hot bath and something to eat, you'll feel better.'

'Not as long as you're around,' Glory breathed.

His arms tightened round her. 'You're unhurt. That's all that matters—'

He contrived to carry her all the way back into the villa and right up the stairs with only the most minor irregularity in breathing. In the mood she was in, she would have preferred it if he had been winded and forced to abandon the macho stance and put her down. As it was, he deposited her on the chaise longue in the bathroom and proceeded to run water into the jacuzzi.

'Get in, *cara*…' Rafaello prompted when the bath was ready for her. Barefoot, his trousers drenched to the knees, his black hair tousled by the wind and his aggressive jawline darkened by a blue-black shadow of stubble, he was a far cry from his usual elegance.

She was ashamed that he still seemed wildly attractive to her. 'Only when you get *out*.'

His eyes flared gold. 'I'm not leaving you alone. You might faint—'

'You're too used to little, fragile women who get off on

big, strong men looking after them. I *don't*. It's your fault I went out in a storm to get away from you!'

Without further argument, Rafaello just picked her up and settled her into the jacuzzi. She sat in the water still wearing his shirt and stared down into the bubbles sent up by the jets. Her strained eyes were suddenly prickling with tears.

'If I've got you pregnant I'll marry you,' Rafaello asserted harshly.

Glory was stunned. She could feel her heart racing but almost as quickly it slowed and sank again. He wasn't serious, he could *not* be serious. Rafaello Grazzini marry the gardener's daughter just because he had got her in the family way? He sounded like a male being roasted on a fire to breaking point, and his tone spoke volumes for his true feelings. It was a reluctant proposal, powered by guilt. In terms of class, she was hardly his equal. He had to be cringing at the mere thought of having to take a wife from a background as humble as hers was. 'You can forget that option. I would never be *that* desperate,' Glory responded flatly, striving to sound wholly unimpressed by an offer that had momentarily made her foolish heart leap with joy. She played fair. He didn't love her. She knew better than to snatch at an impulsive proposal made for all the wrong reasons.

'I made the mistake. I take full responsibility for it. I'm sorry,' Rafaello ground out half under his breath.

'Sorry enough to let me go home tomorrow?' Glory whispered tightly, not looking at him, sick with disappointment that his last words should have totally confirmed what had prompted that surprising offer of a wedding ring.

The silence simmered.

'No…not that sorry,' Rafaello qualified in the most ludicrous tone of apology.

She hunched her shoulders. 'What are you getting out of this?'

'You.'

She rested back against the padded pillow surround and let the water jets buffet her weary body with warmth and relaxation. She had never felt so tired in her life. When she surfaced from her inexorable drift into sleep she was out of the bath, propped up against Rafaello, and he was stripping off the wet shirt. Before she could object he had folded her into a giant, soft towel.

'You can't see it now but we're going to be great together, *bella mia*,' Rafaello told her with stubborn conviction. 'When you wake up tomorrow the sun will be shining and you'll feel different.'

Unresponsive in her exhaustion, Glory sank into the wonderful comfort of the bed.

'You need to eat,' Rafaello told her.

'I couldn't.' She did not think she had the strength to lift a knife and fork. Her drowsy gaze flickered over the exquisite miniature portraits set into the headboard of the bed. 'Who are they?'

'Saints. Those are icons.'

Glory dealt him a shaken look. 'What are you doing with a bed with saints watching over it?'

'It's a Corfiot marriage bed. It belonged to my mother's family.'

Glory had forgotten that his late mother had been an Italian raised in Corfu. 'A marriage bed?' So dismayed was she by the thought of how inappropriate that choice of venue had been for an unwed couple that her superstitious nature came to the fore. 'We should never have been in it!'

'It's just a *bed*, Glory.' Viewing her with wondering dark eyes, Rafaello slowly shook his head at that comment.

Throwing him an exasperated glance that implied that he was downright stupid not to appreciate the natural order of things, Glory closed her eyes and went to sleep, but not before she had said her prayers.

Just as Rafaello had promised, Glory woke to sunshine.

She was alone in the bed and there was no telling dent in the pillow beside her own. She headed straight into the shower to wash out the sand still clinging to her hair. Wrapped in a towel, she emerged again to find that a maid was unpacking her case. Choosing a blue skirt and a white sun-top, she went back into the bathroom to get dressed.

The door she had left ajar was slowly pushed wider.

'Breakfast?' Rafaello stood on the threshold, heartbreakingly handsome in a black T-shirt and well-cut chinos.

'I could eat a horse,' Glory admitted, colour rising in her cheeks, her eyes not quite meeting his.

The table on the balcony beyond the bedroom was laid with an extravagant choice of breakfast dishes. Glory took a cushioned seat and reached for the jug of orange juice. In silence she then worked her way through a bowl of cereal.

Rafaello studied her with brilliant dark eyes that probed her evasive gaze. 'We start fresh today.'

'Do we?' Honey-blonde head downbent, Glory sampled two of the cooked dishes on offer and the toast. Fresh? As though last night had never happened? Was he joking? An intimate ache new to her experience was sufficient reminder of the intimacy they had shared. However, she was infinitely more worried about the risk of pregnancy. While she had been in the shower, counting and recounting the days of her cycle had given her no comfort. Rafaello had made love to her at what was supposed to be the optimum time for a woman to conceive. An even greater concern was her own inexplicable, bone-deep conviction that what she most feared had already happened and that right now deep down inside her tiny cells of human life were engaged in frantic baby-making activity.

'Glory…' Rafaello reached out and ensnared her fingers before she could reach for another slice of toast. 'Did you fast before you arrived? Or are you now eating for two?'

Slowly Glory raised her head, bright blue eyes stricken in her pale oval face. 'Is that really your idea of a joke?'

Rafaello sighed. 'I know the way your mind works, *bella mia*. You took one look at those icons on the bed last night and primitive superstition felled you right before my eyes—'

'I do not have primitive superstitions!' Glory snapped.

'No? If there had been a church within walking distance you'd have been in it all night on your knees,' Rafaello groaned in rueful amusement. 'Are you listening to me? We did nothing wrong...'

Compressing her lips, Glory dropped her head.

'And no dire punishment is about to come your way,' Rafaello continued with unshakable conviction. 'I doubt that there will be repercussions from a single encounter.'

'Got a hotline to mother nature too, have you?' Glory could not resist saying.

Thrusting back his chair, Rafaello reached for her hands and hauled her up into the circle of his arms. 'You're the most appalling pessimist. Do you remember that picnic we had years ago? You kept on saying that it was such a gorgeous day that it was sure to rain. I couldn't quite grasp that connection—'

'It *did* rain,' Glory reminded him, recalling that midsummer afternoon five years before when everything between them had seemed almost frighteningly perfect. Within forty-eight hours they had parted. 'It rained when we were on the way back to the car.'

'So you took the edge off the whole occasion, fretting about something you couldn't control?' Rafaello pushed up her chin and stared down at her mutinous face with dark golden eyes that sought and held hers. 'That's a waste of time and energy. Whatever happens, I'll look after you.'

In receipt of those particular words, Glory shivered. So she was superstitious, so she believed in ESP. She noticed that he was no longer assuring her that he would marry her, had naturally thought better of that rash statement. No doubt he was already grateful that she had not accepted his proposal. She was tempted to ask what 'looking after' would entail but suspected that she already knew the answer. When a guy also used terms like 'repercussions' and 'dire punishment' as euphemisms for pregnancy he was telling her far more about his own attitude than he realised. Very probably he would suggest that a termination would be the wisest solution. No way, not *her* baby, Glory thought fiercely.

But there was no denying that she did suffer from that innate belief that every wrong action was followed by a kind of retributive balancing act. Even so, it was plain crazy for her to be imagining that she might be pregnant within hours of making love, wasn't it? Once again, Rafaello was right. Conception was not an event she could influence. What was the point of worrying herself to death at this stage?

'Finish your breakfast,' Rafaello advised. 'It's a treat to be with a woman who has a healthy appetite.'

An involuntary laugh tumbled from her. 'I couldn't manage another bite…'

'Nor could I—'

'You haven't eaten,' she protested.

'I breakfasted while you were still asleep.' The dark timbre of his voice had taken on a husky edge.

A lean hand splayed across her hipbone. She collided with his amazing eyes. Hot, sizzling gold. The wild flare of sensual awareness made her tense. Her mouth running dry, it was she who moved closer, charged by her own shameless yearning. She stared up into that lean, strong face, reacting to the explosive tension and the weakening surge of heat awakening deep in her pelvis.

A shimmering smile of satisfaction slashed his beautiful mouth and she trembled. Her face burned as he let his hands slowly mesh into the fall of her hair, tipping back her head, letting his thumbs caress her earlobes, making her shiver. 'I could not have trusted myself in that bed with you last night,' he confided.

'No?' Glory snatched in an audible breath, so entirely in thrall to the magnetic spell of his sensual power that she was lost.

'You deserved a night of undisturbed rest, so I slept next door and I tossed and I turned and I had a cold shower around dawn.'

'Masochist?'

'A necessity. The very thought of you makes me *ache...*' Rafaello told her hoarsely, his breath fanning her cheek, his mouth taking hers in a hot, hungry surge of cruel brevity before he lifted his proud, dark head again. Linking his hands with hers, he drew her slowly back into the bedroom.

Glory was all of a quiver, shaken at how fast and how easily he could turn her from rational thought. It was as if her body had a fever that only he could assuage, but no longer did she try to deny that craving. She loved him and accepting that love had only made the wanting all the more powerful a force. She had been wrong, so wrong about its being a cold, callous arrangement, she told herself. Last night he had searched for her, shown his concern and his regret. That was enough, that was truly enough to silence her worst misgivings. Nobody got everything, she argued with herself. Lots of folk had to settle for less than what they had once hoped to receive.

'What are you thinking about?' Rafaello demanded as he drew her, unresisting, down onto the bed with him.

'Nothing...' Glory let her hands rise up over his warm, muscular torso in an exploratory foray that was her very first. He stretched like a lithe tiger being stroked, brilliant eyes narrowing in slight surprise. As he bent his head a secretive smile as old as the Sphinx curved her ripe mouth. However long it lasted, he would remember her *always*, she swore.

As if sharing that identical ambition, Rafaello ran his expert mouth down the extended length of her throat, and her entire body hummed on the gasp of response that he dragged from her. Even the feel of him, hard and ready through the barrier of their clothes, sent the flame inside her leaping higher and proceeded to make her melt. But settling for less, she decided on the peak of another tormenting assault on her sensitised skin, could well mean receiving more pleasure than she had ever dreamt possible...

Glory studied the exquisite silver and turquoise choker in the mirror and then her bright eyes widened to take in the whole of her reflection. She did not recognise that elegant, classy lady as herself.

In the space of three weeks, her appearance had been transformed. She had swallowed her pride and allowed Rafaello to buy her clothes. Why? She had very wounding memories of never, ever having had the right clothes when she was seeing him five years earlier. Telling herself then that such superficial things shouldn't matter had been cold comfort when she stuck out like a sore thumb in company. Neither she nor her friends had owned the kind of outfits worn by the women who were part of Rafaello's world: the casual but oh-so-smart separates, the fashionable but understated garments that none the less screamed their designer tags. She had been tortured by fears that her appearance and her visible inability to blend in was an embarrassment to him.

Now sheathed in a Versace dress, purchased from one of the designer outlets that Corfu town offered the rich who flocked to the island over the summer, she had no such fear. The sleek dress was a magical shade somewhere between green and blue and with every movement and change of light the wonderful fabric seemed to change colour. It made her feel like a million dollars and gave her confidence.

Her thick mane of hair had been tamed and styled to fall back from her face. While she was in that exclusive salon she had taken advantage of the opportunity to be made up and had watched and learned and bought everything that was used with the gold credit card Rafaello had given her. So now she knew all about highlighting her cheekbones and using a subtle glimmer of different shadows on her eyelids. What had amused her most was the discovery of just how much work was involved in attaining that sun-kissed and wholly deceptive natural look.

Silver drop earrings with turquoise inserts hung from her ears. A silver watch encircled her wrist. Now Rafaello was set on buying her an elaborate choker. He had tried to tempt her into gold and diamonds and she had just laughed. She loved silver, and when she left she could take the silver jewellery with her without feeling bad about it, for on his terms such items cost next to nothing even in the most expensive shops. But there would be precious memories bound up in her possession of every piece. Memories she would share with their child on some distant day in the future. Her lovely face shadowing at a reality she had only had confirmed beyond doubt the day before, Glory thought back to the daunting but telling exchange she had shared with Rafaello several days earlier...

That particular morning, she had wakened feeling off-colour. As her period had already been slightly overdue, the nausea she was experiencing had reawakened her fear that she might be pregnant but she had decided that there was no point in involving Rafaello in her worries before there was any actual proof. After all, she had heard friends say that even a change of climate or a different diet could interfere with a woman's cycle.

However, when Rafaello had teasingly called her lazy for lying in bed so late, stress had provoked Glory into a

snappish reply. 'Look, I'm just not feeling that great...
OK?'

'Is it that time of the month?' Rafaello had queried with
a frown, his sudden tension pronounced.

By putting her on the spot like that before she knew how
matters stood herself, he had disconcerted and embarrassed
her. 'Probably...yes...' she had responded hurriedly, pick-
ing up on his tension and telling herself that in all likelihood she *was* worrying herself unnecessarily.

'Well, that's good news, isn't it?' Rafaello had commented with a brilliant smile that seemed to accentuate his
relief with cruel efficiency. 'At least you're not pregnant,
bella mia.'

Once he had made that assumption and once she had
witnessed his relief, wild horses could not have dragged the
real truth from her. Forty-eight hours afterwards she had
made a covert visit to a doctor in town and had learned
that she was indeed in the very early stages of pregnancy.
In choosing not to tell Rafaello, she had made the right
decision, she told herself bracingly. Neither marriage nor a
termination was on the cards and no way would she put
him through the hypocrisy of attempting a supportive role
in a pregnancy which he had so patently *not* wanted to
happen. That would hurt her too much. After all, what did
she really have left but her pride?

'Glory...?' The laughter in Rafaello's dark, deep drawl
dragged her back to the present.

Pasting a determined and bright smile back onto her
downcurved lips, Glory finally turned away from the shop
mirror.

'I gather you like it.' Rafaello sent her a vibrant smile
of amusement and she realised that, having interpreted her
long silence as sheer appreciation, he had already paid for
the choker.

'It's really beautiful.

But not one quarter as beautiful as him, Glory reflected

helplessly, scanning his lean, dark, devastating face with dreamy eyes of appreciation. Not once in five years had she known such happiness as she had experienced with him in recent weeks. She could not bring herself to destroy what had been a time of enchantment with the brutally realistic and unwelcome announcement that she was going to have his baby.

So if she was a bit sad now it was only to be expected. What goes around comes around. She had been right, he had been wrong and, whether he knew it or not, their time together was slowly running out. Her body was already changing with pregnancy. The speed of that development filled her with both fascination and fear. Her breasts were tender and the mere smell of certain foods made her nauseous. But surely she could manage to conceal those facts for another few weeks?

Linking sure fingers with hers, Rafaello walked her down the steep steps outside the shop and back into the colourful lively crowds passing through the narrow street. She adored Corfu town: the legacy of tall Italianate buildings adorned with shutters and balconies left behind by four centuries of Venetian rule, the buzz of the streets and cafés, the array of fascinating shops filled with silver, olive wood, needlework and leather-craft items. Even the locals came out to promenade round their town during the long evenings.

'I suppose now we head for your favourite place,' Rafaello commented lazily.

'If you don't mind...'

A Frenchman had built the Liston as a copy of the Rue de Rivoli in Paris. The arched façade filled with fashionable cafés overlooked a lush green cricket pitch surrounded by trees. She adored sitting there to watch the world go by with Rafaello by her side.

'Why do people keep on staring at us?' she had asked uncomfortably on her first visit.

'You are a very beautiful woman.' His amused but appreciative smile that she should even ask such a question had dissolved the insecure feelings she always struggled to hide from him and made her heart sing. She had a desperate need to believe that she *could* look like the sort of woman who belonged with him.

While Rafaello ordered wine for himself Glory pored over the ice-cream menu to make her selection. Then she rested back in her comfortable seat to survey him, torn between pain and pleasure. He was a visual joy to her from the crown of his gleaming dark head to the soles of his feet. Nothing about him jarred. She was so much in love with him, she could have shouted it from the rooftops. But, denied that outlet, she burned with inner intensity and quailed in torment at the prospect of tearing herself from him.

Suppressing that miserable awareness, Glory made herself dwell instead on the wonderful days they had shared and the endless nights of mutual passion. One day drifting into the next, seamless, timeless, marred by only the rarest disagreement and resealed by the fastest reconciliations on record. He had taught her to swim but had made several biting comments when he finally realised that she *still* preferred drifting round the villa pool in a large plastic ring like an overgrown child or just sitting at the foot of the Roman steps, submerged but safe. Only when he had appreciated the fear of deep water that she had overcome initially only for his benefit had he appreciated the level of her achievement. He thought her ring was cute now. He didn't laugh when she just paddled down on the beach either.

She would carry away memories of wandering through the cool, shaded orchards that surrounded the villa, endlessly talking while they picked a path through the lush green trees laden with velvety peaches, tangerines and cherries beneath the burning blue sky. She would remember the glittering white of the sand-dunes at noon and the dark atmospheric richness of the church dedicated to the island's revered St Spyridon. But most of all she would cherish the reality that he had never once called her his mistress or treated her with anything less than respect.

'If you don't start talking soon about what's bothering you, *cara mia*,' Rafaello murmured with his lustrous dark golden eyes fixed to her with magnetic probing force, 'I'm likely to get annoyed with you.'

Glory froze as if he had turned a gun on her, dismayed that her façade of contentment had not been as good as she had imagined. It really shook her that he had evidently noted a change in her behaviour.

'Not *that* annoyed,' Rafaello groaned with rueful amusement.

'I just don't know why you should think there's anything bothering me,' Glory said tautly and she shrugged for good measure, but one of her hands had found its way down to her still flat tummy under the table.

'You are not a naturally silent woman but for the last few days it's been as though you're not quite with me any more, *mia preziosa*. So what's wrong? Is it your family? You never mention them but possibly that's because you're missing them.' Rafaello regarded her expectantly.

Glory turned scarlet with discomfiture. She never mentioned her family, not only because she could not bear to recall the arrangement that had brought her out to Corfu in the first place but also because she dreaded any further reference to that five thousand pounds which had branded her as mercenary in his estimation.

'If you're discreet I don't see why you shouldn't phone them,' Rafaello proffered with the air of a male making a generous gesture.

'But...but I've been calling them every few days since I got here,' Glory admitted in some bewilderment.

Rafaello tensed in evident shock.

Glory frowned. 'I didn't think you'd mind. I didn't stay on the phone long.'

'Let me get this straight,' Rafaello breathed in a charged undertone, golden eyes smouldering. 'Even though I asked you to be discreet, you have been chattering your dizzy head off to your father and your brother every few days?'

Glory paled and stiffened and then slowly nodded, wondering why on earth he was looking so angry.

Rafaello vented a single foreign word that sounded as though it might be a rude word.

Glory gulped and wondered if her own excusable omissions lay at the heart of his annoyance. Feeling horribly guilty, she muttered, 'You know, I never thanked you for being so very kind to Sam...I just didn't want to discuss all that stuff that happened. I'm sorry, I—'

'Shut up,' Rafaello urged not quite levelly, evidently striving to get a grip on his temper and not one whit cooled by her sincere offering of gratitude. Almost simultaneously he rose from his seat, tossed some banknotes down on the table and strode down the steps to await her.

Her own temper rising, Glory moved to join him at slow-motion speed.

'Have you the *smallest* conception of what you have done?' Rafaello ground out in a raw undertone.

'Don't you talk to me like I'm a brick short of the full load!' Glory warned him in a sideways hiss.

'I hate to state the obvious, *bella mia*...' Rafaello countered grittily, grasping her hand and resisting all her covert attempts to pull free of his hold '...but if you have cheerfully let your family know that you're out here shacked up with me—'

'Of course I haven't done that!' Glory snapped even as pain stabbed her at his use of that particular description of their relationship.

Rafaello stopped dead and turned to survey her. 'You...*haven't*?'

'Dizzy I may be sometimes but not downright thick. You think I'm proud of being here with you? Well, you think

wrong and I'd be *ashamed* to let my father or my brother
know how low I've sunk!' Glory completed in a shaking
but fierce undertone.

Rafaello stared at her, his fabulous bone-structure prom-
inent beneath his bronzed skin, his hard gaze darker than
the blackest night. He said nothing and it was Glory who
turned away first and began walking back in the direction
of the car again. She was feeling sick. Her legs didn't feel
strong enough to hold her upright either.

He unlocked the passenger door of the car first. She
climbed in, her lovely face pale as marble and as expressionless, but inside herself she was just dying. She had not
meant to say all that but he had hurt and provoked her. He
swung in beside her and the horrible silence pulsed.

She laced her hands together to stop them trembling.
'Dad and Sam just think I've moved and they haven't asked
the address because they don't write me letters. They assume I'm using a public phone with a number they can't
call me back on. I didn't have to tell any lies,' she explained in tight voice. 'Neither of them has ever visited me
in Birmingham, so they don't really have much curiosity
about my life there.'

'I'm sorry. I misunderstood,' Rafaello breathed with icy
cool, but there was an underlying roughness to his accented
drawl. 'I employ your father. I thought your brother was a
decent kid. I asked you to be discreet for *their* sake and
yours, not my own.'

'No point advertising that you're slumming on a temporary basis, is there?' Glory heard herself say nastily. 'After all, now you've dressed me up in the designer togs,
nobody could possibly tell that you took me off a factory
floor!'

If the previous silence had pulsed, the one that followed
that blunt and inflammatory response fairly sizzled. Again
Rafaello said nothing, which really infuriated her. She
knew she would have been better saying nothing too but

entire speeches that would rip him to shreds were trembling in readiness on the tip of her tongue and holding them back tortured her. He drove off. She would have liked him to grate through the gears and jerk the wheel to demonstrate emotional upset but he drove as if he had just come through an advanced driving test with pronounced care and caution.

She kept quiet for a whole ten minutes and then it got too much for her. 'I really *hate* you, Rafaello Grazzini!'

'Naturally you do,' he murmured flatly. 'Sex and debt are hardly a satisfactory basis for any relationship. My choice, my mistake.'

Tears drenched Glory's eyes in a tidal wave. She squeezed her eyes shut, hating herself for tearing away the barriers and leaving them both without defence. But at the same time she was powerfully tempted to kick him. Why was he making things worse? Was he fed up with her, bored already? But what did it matter if he was? Wasn't she leaving anyway? For how could she stay with him when her waistline was going to vanish?

Back at the villa, she locked herself in the bathroom. Ripping off her clothes, she got into the shower and turned it on full so that she could sob to her heart's content. It was an hour before she crept out, eyes stinging from all the cold water she had splashed in them. Mercifully the bedroom was unoccupied. She dug into a drawer for a nightdress, the first she had worn since her arrival, and crawled into bed.

Somewhere in the early hours when she was lying there sleepless, drowning in buckets of self-pity, the bedroom door opened. She froze. She had not bothered to close the curtains and in the clear moonlight she saw a bronzed male silhouette. It was Rafaello, only a white towel knotted round his lean hips. She shut her eyes tight and seconds later noted the slight give in the mattress as Rafaello sank down on it.

She rolled over and arrived on his side of the bed only

a moment after he did. Expelling his breath in a slightly startled hiss, Rafaello closed his arms round her. 'We have to talk…'

Panic assailed Glory, for she did not want to talk. He might not appreciate it but the die was already cast. Nothing could be resolved, nothing could be changed. Gliding up over his lean, hard, muscular body in the circle of his arms, she pressed herself close and found his mouth for herself. For a horrendous instant as he tautened in surprise at the blatant invitation she thought he might push her away. Then, just as suddenly, he reacted by pinning her beneath him and deepening that kiss with a driving hunger that shook her.

In the moonlight he threw up his head again and scanned her with fathomless dark eyes. 'I want you *but*—'

Glory had no desire to hear what came after. Sinking desperate fingers into the black hair still damp from the shower, she drew him down to her again. A throaty groan escaped him but she was stronger when it came to the wiles of a temptress. She knew what he could not resist. She knew what drove him wild. Within minutes he was as much the prisoner of his own hunger as she was and way past rational speech.

There was none of the long, teasing rise to gradual excitement with which they had wiled away many a long afternoon. She had unleashed a storm of fierce passion that was well out of her control. He sank into her with delicious driving force, sent her out of her senses with pleasure, and every time she reached a peak it would all start again. A seemingly endless cycle of raw excitement and ecstatic satisfaction left her drained and rather shell-shocked around dawn, when he finally fell into a much-deserved sleep of exhaustion.

Glory lay beside him, questioning what had been different apart from the silence, and then it came to her: he had been saying goodbye to her. He knew it was over. He had decided that before he even came to bed, probably expecting her to be sound asleep. He wanted out. Only not because he was bored with her or because he no longer desired her. Earlier this evening things had got messy, and Rafaello did not like messy scenes. Perhaps it had finally dawned on him that, far from hating him, she loved him.

And, if he hadn't already guessed just how deep her emotional involvement already went, what had just happened between them would have got the message home to him fast. She had *thrown* herself at him like a brazen hussy. Not in a subtle, seductive way either. She cringed for herself and then swithered feverishly between fear and uncertainty. Stress about being pregnant and her own insecurity could be making her oversensitive, she reasoned. Maybe she was just *imagining* that she somehow knew what he was thinking.

But later that same morning she seemed to receive her answer to that question. Fully dressed, Rafaello wakened her. In a lightweight jacket worn with a dark blue shirt and teamed with faultlessly tailored beige chinos, he looked so gorgeous, he took her breath away.

'I have to go out,' he told her flatly. 'Jack Woodrow called me last week to ask for investment advice and I still haven't taken care of it.'

The first week of her stay Rafaello had taken her over to dine at the Woodrows' palatial villa. The prospect of being entertained by a genuine earl and his wife had made Glory feel quite sick with nerves. However, the scornful Fiona had been nowhere to be seen and the brunette's parents, Lord and Lady Woodrow, had turned out to be a delightful and charming older couple. They had greeted Rafaello with fond affection and welcomed Glory to their summer home without the smallest sign of discomfiture.

Rafaello sent her a veiled glance, his tension pronounced in the hard angles of his strong profile. 'Look, we'll talk when I get back but you should pack. We're flying back to London this afternoon.'

Well, she wasn't hanging around for that denouement, Glory told herself steadily. She would save them both from an embarrassing final encounter followed by an even more painful three-hour flight back home. No doubt he would try to ditch her with courteous consideration. What had got into him five years earlier she would never know, for the callous indifference he had shown towards her feelings then had not been his style.

At her request, Rafaello's manservant, Hilario, took her to the airport an hour later. But as soon as Hilario had departed again Glory got into a taxi and travelled back into town. She had seen several casual jobs advertised in cafés and bars. If Rafaello was leaving Corfu, why should she? Back in England, she no longer had either a home or a job. Furthermore, she had very little money. Nor could she face the prospect of returning to the gardener's cottage on the Montague Park estate. Her pregnancy would distress and embarrass her father a great deal and gossip might even carry the news of her condition right back to Rafaello. No, she was on her own and it was time she got used to that idea again...

CHAPTER SEVEN

STANDING beneath the awning that shaded the empty tables in the narrow alleyway, Glory took the opportunity to rub at the small of her back where the ache was worst. Late afternoon the bar attracted little passing trade, but no matter how quiet it was she was not allowed to sit down.

Eight weeks had passed since Glory had walked out of Rafaello's villa to save face. She had soon lived to regret that impulsive decision, for nothing had gone quite as she had planned. Renting a room in Corfu town had proved to be much more expensive than she had naïvely expected and she had used up all the money she had before she had finally got a job as a waitress. Indeed she had only recently managed to save up enough to cover the purchase of an air ticket back to London.

In addition, now that the summer crowds of tourists were thinning, temporary bar staff were being laid off, so she was unlikely to have a job for much longer. When she finally flew back to England she would still be very short of cash. Staying on in Corfu had not been a good idea. Back home she would have had a better chance of finding employment while she did not look pregnant, she reflected ruefully. Now she could only get into trousers with elasticated waists and her once flat tummy was beginning to protrude, no matter how hard she tried to hold it in.

So why had she let Rafaello escape the consequences of their short-lived affair? In retrospect, her own behaviour seemed foolish and short-sighted. Recognising his tension that day when he had asked her whether she was feeling unwell because it was that time of the month, she had said yes out of an instinctive need to lessen his obvious concern.

Unfortunately, her recognition of his relief in receipt of the premature reassurance had sealed her fate and left her with the pretence to maintain. But, naturally, Rafaello had been relieved, Glory told herself miserably. Sex was sex but babies were something else entirely to the average male. She had heard that some men actually got broody just like women did. However, it had seemed pretty obvious that nature had so far left Rafaello untouched by a craving for fatherhood.

But it would have been more sensible for her to have steeled herself and told him the truth: that she was expecting his child and that she intended to have her baby. Why had she felt so guilty about that decision? Even more to the point, why on earth did she miss Rafaello so unbearably? It was madness for her to be missing him when he had been on the brink of ditching her anyway. After just three weeks too. All that romantic holding of hands, all the compliments, the charm, the seemingly insatiable level of his desire for her...and what had all that been worth at the end of the day? Feeling her eyes prickle, Glory blinked back the tears that of late seemed to come all too easily to her. No doubt wiser women than she was had been fooled by men, but how many of them had been taken in *twice* over by the same guy?

Glory suppressed a groan as she thought of the effort she had made and the pride she had dumped just to look classy for him. She should have gone for really tarty clothes and embarrassed the hell out of him every chance she got. That was what he had deserved. But oh, no, Glory Little had acted like a bimbo right to the fall of the final curtain. Remembering how she had passed that last night in Rafaello's bed made her shrink with mortification. Here she was, pregnant, poor, miserable and alone, and she had not even the consolation of knowing that she had told him where to get off!

Out of the corner of her eye she finally registered that

one of the tables at the far end of the bar's pitch had been taken. After two steps in that direction she recognised the angle of that arrogant dark head, the mysterious fluid arrangement of that lithe, lean body that, even seated, contrived to put out an impression of cool command and wealthy exclusivity. Her feet faltered and her heart leapt into what felt like the foot of her convulsing throat.

Rafaello removed his sunglasses. Lustrous, dark deep-set eyes zoomed in on her. His hard jawline clenched. Even wearing that grim and tense expression and clad in what appeared to be a formal business suit, he looked incredibly sleek and sexy.

A seriously debilitating wave of love and lust gripped Glory. She wanted him to smile. Why did he look so bleak? After all, what had she done? Taken herself off without fanfare? Hardly a hanging offence. Indeed, a lot of men would have been grateful to have been spared the inevitable messy and awkward scene of their parting. She tilted her chin but felt the hot betraying colour of awareness flood her cheeks.

'Sit down,' Rafaello suggested.

'I can't. I'm not allowed to,' she said unevenly, wondering wildly if he had missed her too and if he had sought her out to tell her so. Gripped by so much desperate hope that she could no longer look him in the face, she added jerkily, 'What would you like to drink?'

'Either sit down or tell me where you're staying and we'll go there to talk,' Rafaello countered tautly.

'How did you find me?'

'With the greatest of difficulty.' Lines of strain girded his wide sensual mouth as she stole a glance at him from beneath her lashes. 'But Sam was of some help—'

'*Sam?*' His reference to her kid brother in that line bewildered Glory.

'Glory...I have news that you are likely to find distressing.'

Her own fantasy that he might be making an approach to persuade her back to him burned into her soul like acid. By no stretch of the imagination could he believe that such a proposition would qualify as 'distressing'.

'Nothing you could tell me would distress me, and if you don't want a drink I'm not hanging around here to chat.' Employing that scornful assurance in an effort to conceal her own pitiful sense of disappointment, Glory began to turn away again.

'*Santo cielo!*' Rafaello gritted in a driven undertone and he thrust back his chair to rise to his full commanding height. 'Your father is ill…'

Glory jerked into the stillness of complete shock and gaped at him.

'I'm here to fly you home so that you can be with him,' Rafaello explained, temper back under control again, his voice level and quiet.

Her skin had turned damp and chilled and her head was starting to swim. She blinked at him. 'Ill with…what?'

'He had a brain tumour,' Rafaello admitted after a pronounced hesitation. 'He…'

Horror engulfed Glory. *A brain tumour?* Dizziness swept over her and, as she lurched towards one of the seats with the belated intent of sitting down, everything blacked out and she fainted.

Surfacing with a muzzy head again, Glory discovered that she was lying on the narrow bed in her room on the floor above the café. Her employer's wife was chattering excitably to Rafaello in Greek and nodding with approval as though impressed by his responses. Her dad was *dead*, Glory recalled with stricken recoil. That was the news that Rafaello had been trying to break gently to her, only obviously he had not wanted to make that announcement in a public place.

'Did Dad just go like Mum did? Suddenly?' Glory whispered sickly.

Rafaello wheeled round, his brow indented with a frown. 'Your father's *not* dead,' he assured her immediately. 'He's had surgery, major surgery. He's holding his own...just.'

Pale as parchment paper, Glory attempted to follow that explanation but her brain was slow to comprehend, for she was numb with shock. She had reacted to Rafaello's arrival on a very personal level, only to discover that he had sought her out again for another reason entirely. She felt completely disorientated. 'Dad's...alive?'

'Yes, but I'm afraid he hasn't recovered consciousness as yet.'

'I was talking to him on the phone only a few days ago,' Glory protested as she pushed herself up on her elbows and sat up.

Rafaello sank down on the edge of the bed so that they were on a level. His brilliant dark eyes were very serious. 'It happened very fast and with little apparent warning. Your father developed a severe headache and simply collapsed. Sam called an ambulance and he was rushed to the local hospital and from there to a larger facility where scanning equipment was available.'

'But the medics operated, so there's hope,' Glory said, more for her own benefit than his. 'That's what I've got to concentrate on.'

'I'll wait downstairs.' Rafaello slid upright again. 'If you can pack quickly we can be in London by late evening.'

Glory was frantic with concern for her father but she appreciated the fact that Rafaello had not offered her empty reassurances. She knew that he was afraid that her parent might not survive the night.

'Did you have business over here?' Glory asked on the drive to the airport, belatedly wondering how he had become involved in the situation.

'No. I came for you. Sam could only tell me that you were working somewhere in this town in a bar. I put my staff on the phones. Bar owners rarely register casual workers and only personal enquiries were likely to receive an honest response.'

'I should have given Sam my address. I'm so sorry,' Glory mumbled, appalled by the trouble and inconvenience he had been put to in his efforts to locate her. He had flown all the way out to the island purely for her benefit.

'I flew out on spec, hoping that you would be traced by the time I arrived. Jon Lyons struck lucky when I was half-way here,' Rafaello completed, tight-mouthed.

Gritty tears lashed the backs of Glory's eyes. Willing them back, she thanked him again and fell silent. He had to be furious with her and she could not blame him. Grateful though she was that he had found her, she was recognising once again that unfortunate extra dimension to her relationship with him. He was her father's employer and the Grazzinis had always prided themselves on being good to their employees. Sam was only sixteen and someone had had to take responsibility in the crisis. It cut her to the bone that the adult forced to take that no doubt unwelcome responsibility had been Rafaello.

She fell asleep during the flight. Rafaello wakened her about an hour before the jet landed and she went to freshen up. When she returned a meal awaited her, and although she had small appetite she did her best to eat in the hope that food would give her more energy. But never had Glory felt more miserable. Even in the midst of fretting about her father, she was horribly conscious of the change in Rafaello's attitude to her. While being concerned, polite and in every way supportive, he was also maintaining a detached and impersonal approach.

'I can manage to get to the hospital on my own,' Glory said tightly as soon as they arrived in London. 'Thank you. You've been wonderful.'

'I'm coming with you. Try to persuade Sam to take a break. He's exhausted,' Rafaello urged. 'You'll also find my housekeeper keeping a vigil by your father's bed—'

'Maud Belper?' Glory glanced at him in surprise.

'I understand that Archie asked her to marry him last week.' Registering her astonishment at that information, Rafaello sighed. 'I gather Sam didn't keep you up to speed on what was happening on the homefront.'

He guessed right, but when Glory thought that development over it became less of a surprise to her. Her father and Maud Belper had known each other all their lives. If long-standing friendship had finally warmed into something more, she ought to be happy for them both. After all, her parent had been a widower for a long time, she reasoned, striving not to feel hurt and excluded at the news that her father had decided to remarry without even mentioning his plans to her. But then, why should he have done otherwise? For a long time she had lived only on the periphery of her father's life.

She looked at Rafaello but only when he was not looking at her. It struck her that his hard-boned features had fined down since she had last seen him. He was so tense as well. He was obviously hating every moment of their enforced proximity, she thought painfully.

'I'm so sorry about all this,' she muttered as she hurried into the hospital lift in advance of him.

As the lift doors whirred shut, Rafaello surveyed her with impenetrable dark eyes, his lean, strong face taut. 'Please don't misunderstand me when I say that I don't feel comfortable with your gratitude. You don't owe me any apologies either. I did what I had to do. It wasn't much. Let's leave it at that.'

Glory lowered her wounded gaze to the floor. She so badly wanted to feel his arms around her again but she knew that that was not going to happen. A gulf the challenging depth and width of an ocean now separated them. Sam was in the waiting room. He rushed to greet her with relief but the whole time he was hugging her his every conversational sally was addressed over her shoulder to Rafaello.

'I can't believe that you got back here with Glory so fast!' Sam was saying. 'I knew you said you would but I thought there would be delays and stuff. Most of the time I've just let Maud sit with Dad—'

'I'd like to see him,' Glory slotted into her brother's fraught flood of speech.

'Maud will have to come out,' Sam told her. 'Only one person is allowed by his bed in the ICU. There just isn't the space for more.'

Rafaello vanished from the doorway.

'He'll sort it,' Sam muttered, his lanky length sagging into a weary slouch. 'He's done everything. Dad would be dead right now if it wasn't for Rafaello. Did he tell you that the surgeons here said they couldn't operate on Dad?'

'No...'

Her brother explained that the only surgical procedure capable of giving their father a fighting chance of survival had not been done in the UK before. Rafaello had had to fly in a top-flight neurosurgeon from New York to perform the operation. This was the same guy who could not stand to be thanked, Glory reflected wretchedly. Rafaello had moved heaven and earth to help her and her family.

Ushered into the ICU by a kindly nurse, Glory focused on her father and all the machinery surrounding him and then breathed in deep. She stopped thinking about herself and her own problems and started praying instead and willing the older man to come through. Around dawn her father's vital signs began showing a marked improvement and, revitalised by that information, Glory went in search of her brother.

But it was Maud Belper who hurried forward when she entered the waiting room, Maud, whose existence Glory had entirely forgotten. In a guilty rush at that awareness, Glory shared the good news. Tears of release from severe stress swam in the older woman's red-rimmed eyes. She gripped Glory's hand. 'Would you mind if I went back in for a while?'

'No, I've been very selfish. Go ahead,' Glory encouraged. 'Where's Sam?'

'Mr Grazzini took him back to his city apartment. Sam was out on his feet. Will you phone them?' Maud begged, her impatience to be back by the side of the man she so obviously loved palpable.

Lingering only long enough to pass on the phone number, Rafaello's housekeeper disappeared. Glory called. Rafaello answered almost immediately and agreed that her news was wonderful but he also insisted that Sam should be left to sleep for as long as possible. She was taken aback by that insistence on the score of her own brother but was too drained to argue. Curling up in a corner seat, she waited out what remained of the night hours.

Mid-morning, Rafaello brought Sam back to the hospital. By then the general prognosis was that Archie Little was on the road to recovery. He had regained consciousness, squeezed Maud's hand and recognized his daughter with a weak smile. As Sam hurried off to take her place by his father's side, Rafaello studied Glory. 'You can come back to my apartment now and sleep—'

'No, thanks,' she said tightly.

'Don't make this more difficult than it already is,' Rafaello told her with a look of reproof. 'Are you planning to kip on a park bench just to score against me?'

Glory folded her arms with a jerk. She was so close to tears, she could not trust herself to speak. She felt frankly surplus to everyone's requirements. From the doorway of the ICU she had watched her father look at Maud's wan but smiling face and had appreciated that he took much greater strength and comfort from the older woman's presence than from hers. Then there was Sam, rushing in beside Rafaello, bopping about like a very large, clumsy puppy and then punching Rafaello's shoulder in that exclusive all-male way to bid him goodbye and barely awarding his sister a second glance.

Sam seemed to have succumbed to a severe case of hero worship where Rafaello was concerned. Indeed, Glory was amazed to see Sam, who could be so very reserved with strangers, so relaxed in Rafaello's company. After all, they hardly knew each other. Obviously her father's illness had brought down barriers but Sam was not behaving in what she considered to be an appropriate way. Rafaello was their father's boss, for goodness' sake, not a best mate or a big brother or something!

'I'm not trying to score against a-anybody.' Glory faltered to a charged halt at the rise of the sob that made her stammer.

Rafaello banded an arm round her hunched shoulders, swept up the handbag lying on the seat she had vacated and walked her into the lift. Too busy fighting to keep the tears in check, Glory was rigid for fear that she might suddenly succumb and fling herself against his chest and start sobbing all over him. Her family no longer needed her. They had got used to getting by without her. She was the needy one and Rafaello was busy supporting all of them like a positive saint. Yet he didn't want her thanks and she didn't want to *have* to be grateful. If she couldn't have his love, she wanted nothing to do with him.

Rafaello tucked her into the limo with careful hands. 'You're wrecked. You need rest. Have a good cry if it makes you feel better.'

'Stop being so *nice*!' Glory gasped accusingly, throwing herself over to the far corner of the rear seat and ducking down her head.

Without warning, a pair of lean and very determined hands settled round her waist and dragged her inexorably across the space she had opened between them. Glory loosed a strangled squawk like a chicken on the run from a meat cleaver. Rafaello brought his mouth crashing down on hers and her hormones seemed to erupt like a volcano in response. She went from raging emotional turmoil and tears to raw excitement within seconds. Instantly she was kissing him back, running her hands over his shoulders, his hair, any part of him within reach, and her heart was hammering and breathing was a luxury no longer required.

It felt *so* good to be back in his arms, she had no control, no thought of what she was doing. Only the elemental surge of her own love and desperate hunger guided her. The pleasure was explosive, primal, almost too hot to bear. When he threw back his head and deprived her of that connection she suffered a cruel sense of loss.

Rafaello stared down at her, golden eyes shimmering like bright sunlight in his lean face, dark colour accentuating the fierce slant of his cheekbones, his jawline clenched hard. 'My only excuse is lack of sleep and a low patience threshold. My apologies, *cara*,' he breathed in a gritty undertone. 'But if it happens again, try pushing me away.'

Trembling and disorientated by a similar amount of sleep deprivation, Glory could not meet his gaze. Her cheeks fired up but that final comment of his filled her with rage. Yet *still* she had an almost overwhelming urge to haul him back to her, to lose herself in that wild heat and excitement where she did not have to think but only feel. Her emotions were all over the place. A combustible mix of love and hatred was tearing her apart.

'Are you letting Maud stay here too?' she asked as she entered the penthouse apartment, trying not to gape too obviously at the large expanses of polished floor stretching off in every direction.

'No, I believe she has a sister in Clapham.'

'Then why's Sam staying with you and not with her?' Glory watched him still and tense at that enquiry and her vague sense that something was not quite right was increased by his reaction to what she saw as a perfectly natural question. 'Maud *is* going to be his stepmother—'

Rafaello gave her an expressionless look. 'Maud has scarcely left the hospital since your father arrived there.'

He strode down a wide corridor, thrust open a door into a bedroom and told her where she would find a spare key for the apartment. She felt that he could not wait to get her out of his sight. She relived her own passionate response in his limo and let the tears come, the tears of stress, which she had held back for so many hours. Slumped on the bed, fully clothed, she fell asleep.

Wakening in the afternoon in her crumpled garments, she felt like an itinerant. The *en suite* bathroom was a dream of glossy tiles and spacious luxury but all too many mirrors. She grimaced at her shadowed eyes and tousled hair. A long shower made her feel much more human. A towel anchored round her, she rubbed at the ache in the small of her back. Ever-conscious of her changing shape in recent weeks, she had begun hunching her shoulders, aware that when she practised good posture her swelling stomach was much more obvious. But enough was enough, she decided ruefully, straightening her shoulders with determination as she padded back into the bedroom.

She stopped dead: Rafaello was in the act of walking in through the bedroom door. 'I did knock...I assumed you were still asleep,' he proffered. 'Sam's back and he tells me that your father is asking for you—'

'Honestly?' Glory exclaimed, touched and pleased by that news. Turning away from him, she headed straight for the case sitting at the foot of the bed. 'I'd better get dressed and get over to the hospital.'

She heard Rafaello draw in a sharp breath. A frownline indenting her brow, she glanced at him again. Rafaello was as still as a graven image, his attention fully lodged to his view of her body in profile as delineated by the unforgiving cover of a fleecy towel stretched to capacity.

'*Per meraviglia…*' he breathed raggedly in the simmering silence. 'You look like a fertility goddess.'

As a schoolgirl, Glory had once seen such a statue in a museum. Being compared with an extremely rotund female from prehistoric times was the kind of compliment she would have gone some distance to avoid. Cringing inwardly, her colour rising, she sucked in her tummy in an effort to make it meet her backbone and forced herself to laugh. 'You're not supposed to tell women when they've put on weight, Rafaello. But then, you know how much I enjoy my food and if I want to be big and beautiful—'

'And…pregnant?' Rafaello dragged his stunned gaze from the no longer visible swell and raked it up to her stricken face.

'*Pregnant?*' Glory parroted shrilly, most of her oxygen supply engaged in the effort it took to keep her tummy in. 'Are you nuts?'

'Let's see. Take the towel off and start breathing again!' Rafaello strode forward, looking very much like a guy with a mission to prove his point by any means available.

Glory backed off, aghast. Shorn of the towel, all would be revealed: her vanishing waist, her increasingly Rubenesque curves.

'Glory…I want the truth,' Rafaello growled, intent golden eyes clashing with hers.

Glory swallowed hard.

'The baby has to be mine,' Rafaello continued, fiercely scanning her pale, strained face for answers. 'It's *got* to be! You're at least a few months along.'

'OK…you win,' Glory whispered through compressed lips, and she dropped her head because she could not bring herself to retain visual contact when she told him. 'Or maybe I should say, mother nature won. Yes, of course it's your baby—'

'So why did you go out of your way to convince me that there was nothing to worry about in Corfu? Was that an honest mistake on your part?' Rafaello demanded in a low driven undertone, his dark deep drawl no longer level. 'Did you only discover that you were carrying my child *after* you'd walked out on me?'

'No.' Suddenly Glory was feeling very guilty and confused. 'One of the days I said I was getting my hair done, I also went to see a doctor. It was confirmed then.'

Rafaello absorbed that confession with bleak, dark-as-midnight eyes. 'So why didn't you tell me?'

Tears gritted up her eyes and she blinked furiously. 'You didn't *want* to know—'

'That is not true.' The contradiction was lethally quiet.

'I *saw* how relieved you were when you believed I wasn't pregnant!' Glory argued chokily.

Briefly Rafaello closed his eyes as if he was praying for patience and then he swung away, the bunched muscles of his powerful shoulders betraying the ferocious level of his tension. 'I was relieved because that was not the way I wanted it to happen. History repeating itself…I didn't want it to *be* like that between us—'

'History repeating itself?' Glory echoed, totally at sea as to his meaning.

Rafaello swung back to her, his darkly handsome features clenched hard. 'Something similar once happened in my own family.'

'Oh…' Weak from stress, Glory sank down on the corner of the bed. 'I really didn't know what to do when I found out I'd fallen pregnant. Maybe I have a bad habit of wanting to tell people what I think they want to hear.'

'That's no excuse.' Disconcertingly impervious to that mode of appeal, Rafaello shot her a look of angry derision.

'You're tough enough when you want to be. All over me like a rash one moment and doing a vanishing act the next. But this is something else again, this is my baby too. I would've married you in Corfu but you were quick enough to tell me that you weren't *that* desperate!'

Struck by the revealing rawness of that final sentence, Glory gave him a shaken appraisal. It was almost three months since he had made that offer and he had never mentioned it again. But only now did she see that she had actually hurt and offended him. When he had voiced that grim assurance that he would marry her if she conceived he had been serious, much more serious than she had given him credit for being. And how had she reacted? She asked herself with a sinking heart. Offered what she most desired in the world but believing it was the most grudging of proposals, she had shot him down in flames.

'You're not being fair,' she argued shakily. 'I was angry and upset that night. I honestly didn't believe you were serious! But I have to admit that I still wouldn't want to marry anybody *just* because I was pregnant—'

'Well, what you want and what you get aren't always the same thing in this life,' Rafaello drawled with icy precision. 'But I can assure you that we are getting married just as fast as I can arrange it. We don't have a choice.'

Glory took a very deep breath and then another. Maybe he was just really hopeless at proposing. In fact, he was a walking disaster on that subject, but on this occasion she had no urge whatsoever to utter a stubborn, proud refusal. She loved him to bits and he was the father of her baby and she was very, very willing to be convinced that they could marry and share a future together. Indeed, there was nothing she wanted more but at the same time she did not want Rafaello opting for that choice solely on the basis that she was carrying his child. 'I can't really agree that we don't have any other choice. I just think I need to hear you give me some reasons *why* you think you should marry me—'

'We're in a bloody tight corner!'

Glory was bitterly disappointed by that response. He was gorgeous, he was clever, he was impatient to do 'the right thing' about two decades after so many men had abandoned such moral niceties, but being in a very tight corner was not the kind of reason she so much needed to hear. Were he to say that he still found her madly attractive or even fun company, she would be happily convinced that their marriage would have a chance of success. But then, possibly he did not think or feel either of those things and her being pregnant was truly his *only* motivation in proposing, she conceded wretchedly.

'You want me to help you out, Rafaello? Babies have a *right* to know who their father is—how about that?' Without the smallest warning, Sam's voice broke in on an aggressive rising note that froze both Glory and Rafaello into stillness, for both of them had forgotten that the teenager was in the apartment and neither had noticed that Rafaello had neglected to close the door. 'Why don't you try that one out on my sister? That reason would be a real good laugh for a Grazzini!'

Glory barely had the time to absorb Sam's startling interruption before her brother launched himself off the threshold and literally threw himself at Rafaello. As she had never seen her easy-going brother even lose his temper before, she could not credit the violence that just seemed to explode from him. Sam hurling abusive swear words was another new experience for her and she sat there, rigid with shock at that physical assault, terrified that Rafaello might lose his temper and fight back.

'Sam...please, *no*!' Glory pleaded brokenly, torn apart by guilt at her brother's distress at what he had overheard.

'I trusted you!' Sam shouted at Rafaello. 'I thought you were different from your—'

'I *am.*' Breathing heavily as he finally got a restraining grip on Sam, Rafaello was strikingly pale beneath his bronzed complexion, his strong bone-structure hard-edged, his dark eyes mirroring the reality that Sam's aggression had shocked him every bit as much as it had shocked Glory. 'I was just being a smart-ass, Sam.' Forced to pin her struggling brother against the wall in an effort to cool him down, Rafaello was suddenly talking very fast. 'I *love* your sister…OK? I really do want to marry her!'

Sam's still furious dark gaze was nailed to Rafaello as if he was searching for the proof of those far-reaching reassurances. 'Glory doesn't need you *just* because she's having a baby…'

'No, but I need her,' Rafaello stated with hard conviction.

As Rafaello stepped back and released Sam, Glory could not look at either of them. She was aghast that her brother had overheard their conversation and horribly ashamed that her behaviour and her condition should have upset him to such an extent. Rafaello was equally shaken and naturally he had endeavoured to come up with the *only* sort of response likely to calm Sam down.

'You needn't think I'm apologising for trying to hit you either!' Sam hurled in a last burst of defiance in Rafaello's direction before he backed warily out of the room as though he was still waiting on some form of violent retaliation.

Sam left a silence in his wake that seemed endless.

'I'd better go and talk to him,' Glory muttered tightly.

'No, let him cool off for a while. He's too upset to handle either of us right now. Anyway, your father's waiting for you,' Rafaello reminded her, raking a not quite steady hand through his luxuriant black hair in a gesture that revealed just how shattered he still was by what had occurred. 'I think we need a special licence, *bella mia*—'

Glory squeezed her anguished eyes tight shut. 'Rafaello—'

'We've done enough damage. Sam's right. Every baby has a right to know who his father is,' Rafaello said with a quality of raw regret in his dark deep drawl that cut her sensitive soul to the bone.

And, on that note, he left her.

CHAPTER EIGHT

ARCHIE LITTLE had been moved out of the ICU into a private room.

Maud Belper was waiting outside that room with a troubled look on her face. 'Could I have a word with you before you go in, Glory?'

'Dad's all right, isn't he?'

'Yes, he's doing fine.' The older woman sighed. 'But Archie's taken it into his head that he must talk to you now. It's a lot to ask but, for *his* sake, could you try to stay calm whatever he tells you? He's still very weak.'

Glory stared at her and then nodded, her colour heightening. No matter how hard she tried not to, she resented Maud's interference. She also felt uneasy about the obvious fact that the other woman was already acquainted with what her father wished to discuss with her. In the awkward silence, however, a sudden rueful smile of comprehension flashed across Glory's face and she leant forward and gave the older woman an impulsive hug.

'*Of course*, we haven't yet discussed the fact that you and Dad are going to get married! I'm really pleased for you both. I'm not saying I wasn't a bit taken aback when I first heard,' Glory admitted with her usual frankness. 'But when I saw you and Dad together, and realised just how much you care for each other, I was truly happy for him.'

'You're a dear girl.' In spite of her answering warmth, Maud's tension remained undiminished 'But I can't let you go in there thinking that that's what Archie wants to get off his chest. It's not.'

Glory had no time for mysteries and she had not forgotten Maud's cryptic remarks that night at Montague Park three months earlier. Was the older woman one of those personalities who revelled in making mountains out of molehills and who enjoyed uttering dire hints and warnings? Embarrassed by that suspicion, Glory hurried into her father's room before her future stepmother could say anything more.

Archie Little looked so much better with a little colour in his cheeks. Settling down into the seat by the bed, she smiled at him. 'You're looking good, Dad.'

'I had to see you and get this over with.' Her father released a troubled sigh. 'But I know that what I have to tell you is going to upset you—'

Get what over with? Glory wanted to question, but instead she cradled his hand where it lay on the bedspread between both of hers and tried to soothe him. 'I'm not that easily upset.'

'It's about Sam. Sam…well, Sam's not mine,' her father said haltingly.

Glory kept her widened gaze focused on his anxious expression, convinced she must have misheard him, and then she said uncertainly, 'You mean…Sam's adopted?'

'No. Your mother…' The older man grimaced. 'She got mixed up with another man—'

'You're pulling my leg,' Glory told him in a teasing tone of disbelief. '*Mum*…with another man?'

'You were only a kid of seven when Sam was born,' Archie reminded his daughter heavily. 'For a long time after that your mum and I lived like strangers.'

Even as he said that, Glory's memory was stirred. Only at that prompting did she recall that her mother had shared her bedroom for a while when she was around that age. Her parents had been sleeping apart, she realised in dismay, shaken that until that moment it had never occurred to her to put that knowledge into its adult context and question what that separation had meant. Her tummy muscles clenched. 'But you and Mum were happy,' she heard herself say as if she was still that young child and begging for reassurance. 'I remember you being happy—'

'Later we were again. But Sam is Benito Grazzini's kid and Rafaello's half-brother,' her father framed, tiredness and stress visible now in his lined features. 'I never would have told you, Glory. I didn't want to tell you. I didn't want to hurt you or spoil your memories of Talitha.'

'It's all right…' Glory managed to say but she had to release his fingers because her own hands were trembling.

No, it could not be true. How could her mother, who had preached purity to her own daughter for so many years, have engaged in an adulterous affair? Worse still, given birth to her lover's child? Her mother and Benito Grazzini? Sheer madness! Where had her poor father picked up this crazy story? Was it in his own head? Something to do with the surgery? Was he getting all confused about people and mixed up about the past?

'I forgave her but she never got over the guilt or the fear of you or Sam finding out,' the older man muttered heavily. 'It was one of those things that nobody could've stopped. I was there the first time Benito Grazzini saw her at an estate party. He and your mum…they couldn't take their eyes off each other and that was the start. It went on all that winter.'

Glory was now straining to catch every word and her refusal to credit what she was being told was being challenged. What was it Maud had said to her that night at Montague Park on the subject of how Archie Little would feel about his daughter being involved with Rafaello? 'You're getting into a situation you don't really understand.' She shivered, chilled inside and out. If Benito Grazzini had fathered Sam it meant that her brother was Rafaello's brother too. Was it possible? She did not *want* it to be possible.

'I'm sorry, Glory. I've not been fair to you either.'
'How?'

'When Benito Grazzini made you give up Rafaello when you were eighteen I was pleased because I didn't want the two of you getting together either.'

There was a horrible ring of truth to her father's discomfited admission.

'But how could you bear to keep on working for Benito Grazzini?' Glory asked, struggling to keep her mounting incredulity out of her voice.

'Because I won. I kept your mother,' Archie Little muttered with a rich satisfaction that seemed undimmed by the passage of years. 'He did everything he could to take her away from me but he *lost*!'

Glory blinked at that most unexpected conclusion. She was in so much shock at what she had learned that she simply sat there, staring into space. When she finally parted her lips to speak again she discovered that she had waited too long to do so, for her father had fallen asleep. As it was unthinkable to wake him up and bother him with further questions on such an issue, she lurched out of his room on legs that were wobbling. Maud was waiting outside.

'Dad's asleep...quite happy,' Glory told her stiltedly. 'You knew, you *knew* all along, didn't you?'

'I didn't know for sure about Sam until your father told me this year. But yes, I knew about the rest,' the older woman confirmed wryly, guiding Glory into the greater privacy of the waiting room. 'I've worked at the Park for the best part of thirty years and I've not missed much of what went on there.'

Glory was still in a shattered state of nerves. 'How could Mum *do* that to Dad?'

'I don't think she meant to hurt anybody—'

'He was a married man,' Glory muttered in a shaking undertone. 'And she was married to Dad...'

'I reckon they both paid a steep price for what they did,' Maud sighed. 'Anyway, your mother came to her senses when she fell pregnant. She told Mr Benito to get lost and that was that.'

'Was it? Dad had to bring up another man's child.' Try as Glory could, she could not square the memories of the mother she had loved with the woman who had irresponsibly indulged in an affair that had damaged her marriage, her husband and the whole future of the son she had brought into the world.

'That was Archie's decision. He adored your mother. He felt he'd come off all right.'

'I've been so slow to catch on,' Glory mumbled, momentarily closing her eyes as if willing herself to get a grip on a brain that was shooting in too many directions at once and throwing up far too many different thoughts. 'Rafaello *knows* Sam is his brother—'

'Sam knows too, Glory. When Archie realised that Mr Benito had told *his* son, he decided that he had to tell Sam the truth as well—'

'Everybody knew but me,' Glory whispered thickly. 'I think Rafaello found out that night I was at the Park. His father came to see him—'

'He wouldn't have had much choice. When Rafaello told his dad that Sam Little had been charged with theft it must've put Mr Benito in quite a sweat. So he finally owned up.'

The more the ramifications of what she had learned sank in, the more distraught Glory could feel herself becoming. Parting from the older woman with an embarrassed apology, she left the hospital.

Everything was falling into place for Glory but she shrank from the picture that was emerging. In all likelihood, Rafaello had had a flaming row with his father that evening. He must have been as shocked by the revelation as she was now but he hadn't breathed a word to her, had he? No, he had packed her off back to Birmingham, ensuring that she remained ignorant of that secret connection between her family and his own. Then he had gone down to the gardener's cottage to take a closer look at the brother he had never known he had and had stayed until after midnight...

In fact, the sole point Rafaello had in his favour was that he evidently did want to acknowledge and form a family connection with Sam. Or *did* he? Perhaps events had got out of his control and her own father had accidentally forced that issue by finally telling Sam the truth about his parentage. Once that cat had come out of the bag, there had been no putting it back. No wonder Sam was in such a volatile frame of mind. Yet Sam had also been showing every sign of being delighted by the discovery that he had an older half-brother. As opposed to a sister? A *half-sister*, Glory acknowledged reluctantly, liking even less a distinction that diminished the blood ties between herself and the brother she loved. Was that why Sam had more or less treated Glory like the invisible woman since her return? Stung by that hurtful reality, which she had tried to ignore until that moment, Glory splurged on taking a cab ride back to Rafaello's apartment.

What seemed like the ultimate betrayal finally struck her. Even knowing that there was no way on earth that he could possibly prosecute his own brother, Rafaello had *still* held Glory to the deal they had made. He had still swept her off to Corfu to become his mistress. Not once had he been tempted or even shamed into telling her that her little brother was also his little brother!

But only as Glory made it into the lift in Rafaello's apartment block did she make what was for her the most distressing connection of all. No longer did she need to wonder why Rafaello had been so quick to offer marriage even in advance of discovering that she was pregnant! Regardless of his own feelings, there was a family dimension to be considered now. It was bad enough that their respective parents had had an affair and that Sam should have been the result, but the fallout from Rafaello's getting

Glory into the same condition would be all the greater precisely *because* of that background. Sam had been quick to think the worst and Archie Little would be equally sensitive. The mere suggestion that Rafaello was treating an expectant Glory with anything less than respect would be sufficient to create an all-out war of loathing and resentment where the men in her family was concerned.

As Glory entered the penthouse Rafaello strode out into the hall to greet her. The sheer effect of his stunning dark good looks combined with his lithe, powerful physique hit Glory really hard. He was just so gorgeous. She was out of her league, *way* out of her league and always had been with him. The instant he had mentioned marriage she should've realised that there was something strange going on. Entrapment? He hadn't been joking. A terrible sense of pain and rejection filled her and she blanked him out, fighting to retain control of her seething emotions, but all the time the anger inside her was rocketing.

'Where's Sam?' she demanded, stalking past him into the contemporary lounge. 'I want to talk to him in private.'

'I'm afraid he's gone—'

'I beg your pardon?' Taken aback, Glory spun round.

'Sam has opted to go and stay with his friend Joe's family for the next few days—'

'And you just let him walk out of here in the mood he was in?' Glory prompted in disbelief.

'Sam's already missed the first week of the new school term,' Rafaello pointed out levelly. 'He discussed his plans with your father this morning. Sam will be fine, Glory.'

'I just bet you wanted him gone before I got back!' Glory launched at him furiously.

'Now, what has put you in this mood?' Rafaello mused, shrugging back his wide shoulders and viewing her with enquiring dark golden eyes.

'Can't you guess?' Glory flung him a livid look and she was so mad, so worked up, she couldn't stay still and she walked all the way over to the window before spinning back again. 'Why didn't you tell me that your lousy father seduced my mother and just about wrecked my parents' marriage?'

Rafaello stilled, spiky black lashes semi-screening his keen gaze. 'So you *know*—'

'No thanks to you!' Glory snapped, outraged by that almost calm reaction to a revelation that had virtually torn her apart. 'Just when were you planning to tell me that Sam has rotten Grazzini genes in him?'

Rafaello's gaze shimmered and then flashed. 'Cut it out, *bella mia*...or I might just hit back.'

'I'm not afraid of anything you could have to say. In every way possible your father has caused enormous distress to my family!' Glory condemned.

'My mother had a nervous breakdown when I was thirteen. I never knew why until I found out about Sam three months ago,' Rafaello admitted, shocking Glory into silence. 'She was a very reserved woman. She tried to pretend the affair wasn't happening, but when my father confessed that there was going to be a child she fell apart. Did you imagine that wealth and position protected my mother from being as hurt as your father was?'

'I never thought about her...maybe because I don't ever remember seeing her.' A hectic flush on her cheeks, Glory was momentarily ashamed of the way she had tried to hurl blame without appreciating that, one way or another, everybody involved had suffered. But conceding that point in no way lessened the bitter sense of betrayal she felt.

'My mother never returned to Montague Park and Benito admitted that, but for Sam's existence, he would have sold the estate. Let's face it, between them, my father and your mother made a hellish mess but the only real victim now is Sam,' Rafaello murmured flatly. 'My father always knew that Sam was his son. However, he had *no* idea that Archie knew as well, so he had no choice but to keep his distance.'

'I guess not,' Glory was forced to admit.

'Now that the truth is out, Benito very much wants to get to know Sam,' Rafaello admitted. 'But Sam needs time to adjust to that idea.'

Rafaello had given Glory another shock and one she could have done without. Benito Grazzini wanted to get to know his illegitimate son? Why did the obvious always have to be spelt out to her? For here was yet another powerful reason why Rafaello *had* to marry her. If Rafaello didn't marry her, his father could kiss goodbye to any hope of Sam's warming to him in the foreseeable future. Devastated by that further realisation, Glory tried to shut it out again because she shrank from the challenge of speaking such humiliating thoughts out loud.

Her lovely face tight and pale, her anguished eyes screened, she said hoarsely, 'You found out the truth about Sam that night I was with you but you didn't *tell* me—'

'How could I tell you? At that stage, I believed your father didn't know he'd been raising another man's son,' Rafaello countered in blunt exasperation. 'However, Archie disabused me of that idea the minute Sam went up to bed that evening. He said that, although he might've been willing to tell Sam the truth, he couldn't do it because he didn't want *you* to know that your mother had had an affair!'

'You still should have told me,' Glory retorted stubbornly.

'It wasn't my secret. To be honest, I didn't think your father would *ever* tell Sam, so it would have been wrong for me to interfere,' Rafaello stated with immovable conviction. 'But while we were in Greece Archie decided that if my father could tell me that Sam was my brother then Sam had the right to the same information.'

'But I was *still* left out of it, even by my own family,' Glory said bitterly, struggling to hide her hurt.

'It's not exactly the kind of news people want to break on the phone.'

'And it's certainly not the sort of news *you* were likely to share when you were using Sam and those theft charges to make me agree to become your mistress!' Glory flung back in fierce condemnation.

Rafaello threw back his arrogant dark head and stood his ground in silence.

'Even knowing that there was *no* way on earth you would have let those charges stand against your own half-brother, you went ahead and dragged me into bed!' Glory continued in a rising crescendo. 'How low can a guy sink?'

'If he wants a woman as much as I wanted you… probably even lower,' Rafaello conceded with disconcerting frankness, brilliant dark eyes bleak, hard jawline clenched. 'I am not proud of what I did, *cara*.'

'That didn't stop you, though, did it?'

Pale beneath his bronzed skin, lean, powerful face taut, Rafaello surveyed her steadily. 'I got pretty much what I asked for. You walked out on me again—'

'*You* were about to dump *me*—'

'No, I wasn't,' Rafaello stated.

'Why are you lying about it?' Glory shot at him shrilly. 'You think my being pregnant means you can't be honest any more?'

'No…' Rafaello responded. 'I think your being pregnant means that I'm not going to fight with you. It can't be good for the baby.'

Off-balanced by what struck her as a shockingly smooth and devious sidestepping of the major issues she was striving to confront him with, Glory experienced such a surge of unfettered rage that she felt light-headed. 'Just you leave my baby out of it—'

'It's my baby too—'

Her teeth gritted on that unarguable point. 'You used me in Corfu—'

His expressive jawline took on a more aggressive slant,

his dark eyes suddenly flaring gold. 'Don't you dare try to tell me that you didn't want me. Don't you *dare*.'

'Is that how you excused yourself?' Glory was impervious to that warning intonation and accelerating tension in the air.

'You were the one who needed the excuse. I won't let our parents' mistakes tear *us* apart—'

'How did *I* need an excuse?' The atmosphere was humming, setting up a chain reaction in Glory's own trembling length.

Rafaello strolled closer, all dominant male, all confident threat. 'An excuse to enjoy the passion,' he drawled soft and low and insolent as all get-out. 'I gave you that excuse, that outlet, that freedom. As long as you could blame me for forcing you into that arrangement, you didn't have to feel guilty. You were no unwilling mistress!'

Outmatched by that demanding reminder of her own weakness, Glory turned scarlet, unable to think of anything to hurl back which would not be an outright lie. Infuriated and embarrassed, she tried to brush past him but Rafaello caught her to him. Trapping her struggling slim body into the unyielding strength of his hard, muscular frame, he crushed her mouth beneath his with passionate force. Sensual shock lanced through Glory in a debilitating wave. In the midst of her raging turmoil she felt her own desperate hunger for that physical connection pulling at her with talon claws, but she fought it.

'Don't do this to us,' Rafaello lifted his dark head to demand in ragged appeal. 'Don't make me so mad that I'll say things that will hurt you, *bella mia*.'

Encountering the blaze of those smouldering golden eyes, reacting to that disconcerting note of masculine urgency, Glory was mesmerised into stillness. It was as if he pressed a magic button and the rage went out of her. She quivered, shifting inexorably into closer contact. The magnetic attraction of that lean, powerful physique of his against her own softer feminine curves was immense. She was madly aware of the hard contours of bone and sinew beneath the formal business suit, and the thrusting promise of his undeniable arousal. Between one breath and the next she was lost to temptation, all resistance beaten down by the answering ache of her breasts and the moist heat stirring between her thighs.

'Rafaello…' she muttered in desperation, fighting to call a halt to her own susceptibility.

Rafaello dealt her a scorching smile and hoisted her up into his arms without another word. He carried her out of the lounge. You can't do this, you *mustn't* do this, cried her conscience on a frantic note. But she ignored that inner voice, pushed her face into a wide, solid shoulder, letting her nostrils flare on the familiar scent of him, feeling every skin-cell she possessed switching onto a higher frequency in response. He laid her down on a bed in an unfamiliar room and plucked off her shoes. Straightening with easy grace, he removed his jacket and tossed it aside.

Glory sat up, flushed and stiff. 'We were fighting—'

'This beats the hell out of fighting, *amore mia*,' Rafaello pointed out with husky conviction.

Her hands were shaking and she wound them round her upraised knees while she fought to find the strength to get back off the bed again, reinstate control and common sense. But her defences weren't working, weren't there to call upon. Her whole world had begun to cave in around her when her father had started speaking a couple of hours earlier. The bricks and mortar of her childhood stability had taken a heavy hit. Little memories were still sneaking up out of her subconscious and striking hard: the phone constantly ringing but never answered, her mother taking it off the hook, pacing the floor, back and forth in tortured circles, hands knotted as if she was praying, tears running down her face as she shooed her curious little daughter into the kitchen and suggested she set the table for supper. A woman fighting temptation, a woman craving the man she loved but denying herself. And just as Talitha Little had loved Benito Grazzini, Glory loved his son.

'Forget them...forget *all* of it,' Rafaello urged with angry impatience as if he was attuned to her very thoughts.

But how could she forget when that was *why* he would marry her? Then would she rather do without him? Would pride be any consolation when she denied herself what she most wanted? Rafaello on any terms. Any way she could have him, she conceded painfully, recalling those wanton weeks on Corfu. Any excuse. He knew that but she was only now facing that same fact that pride had a lesser hold on her than he had.

She connected with his blazing golden eyes, sensing his anger, his frustration and mercifully his desire. Desire was there in the smouldering caress of his gaze as it roved over her, lingering on her full mouth, the pouting thrust of her breasts beneath her buttoned cotton top. Even without the fancy frills of the right make-up and the right clothes, he was hungry for her.

'I am so hot for you, I am burning up,' Rafaello growled, throwing his shirt aside, exposing the hard hair-roughened expanse of his muscular torso and the hard bronze slab of his flat stomach.

'Yes.' Acknowledgement escaped Glory's already parted lips in a sighing breath for she was melting just watching him strip. Total weakness, total lack of resistance, that was what she was feeling and it was running through her like a burst dam of susceptibility. With hands that were all thumbs she began to pull at the pearlised buttons on her top. Then, losing patience, she tugged it over her head and emerged in time to see him strip off his boxer shorts. She caught her breath and her mouth ran dry at the potent virile proof of his male hunger for her.

Arrested bright blue eyes pinned to him, Rafaello padded over to the bed and reached for her. He took about five seconds to extract her from her combat trousers. Kneeling on the bed, he pulled her to him and let his tongue slide once, twice into the moist depths of her mouth in an erotic penetration that sent the blood thundering through her veins in helpless response and left her trembling.

'You're so sexy,' she whispered unevenly.

'And you have the most divine body I've ever seen,' Rafaello husked, depriving her of her bra, freeing the ripe swell of her breasts from confinement, shaping his hands to her burgeoning curves with near reverent care.

Is that *all*? she almost asked, needing to be so much more, but that pained thought was as quickly lost in the rush of pleasure induced by his caressing fingers brushing over her distended pink nipples. The sensation was so intense as to be almost unbearable and she shut her eyes in embarrassment as a moan escaped her.

'You're even more sensitive now, *amore mia*,' Rafaello murmured thickly, impatient hands dispensing with her panties and then rearranging her so that she lay fully exposed to his plundering gaze.

In dismay she opened her eyes wide, and she moved her arms to cross them protectively over herself. He caught her hands in his and settled them back either side of her. 'Rafaello!' she gasped strickenly, painfully aware of her changing shape, needing and wanting to conceal those alterations from too close a scrutiny.

'*Dio mio*...you excite the hell out of me,' Rafaello ground out, raw appreciation in the fascinated appraisal he dealt her prone figure, releasing one of her wrists to run a satisfied hand over the slight swell of her stomach and splay his long fingers possessively there. 'Those Grazzini genes you insulted are inside you, part of me, part of you—'

'Pushy genes,' Glory mumbled, not really knowing what to say because his attitude had taken her by surprise.

Rafaello dealt her a scorching smile that sent her vulnerable heart racing. 'Strong and assertive, *cara mia*,' he countered with amused agreement.

He really *did* want their baby. For the first time she recognised that reality and, even as relief coursed through her, it brought pain in its wake, for his warmth seemed directed at the child she carried, rather than at her. His child lay at the very heart of his wish to marry her. So when he kissed her there were tears in her eyes, but when he touched her quivering body she could no longer retain such thoughts. Indeed, she was all the more eager to forget and find the only true oblivion she had ever known.

Excitement took her in a fiery rush as he found the throbbing peaks of her breasts, lowered his proud, dark head and tasted the swollen buds, laving them with his tongue, delicately grazing them with his teeth. He was setting her on fire, rousing a tight aching feeling deep in her pelvis, making her gasp at the slow-burn effect of his knowing touch on a body too long starved of sensation.

'I do want you…I *always* want you!' she moaned in sudden shame at her inability to control the wild hunger he had ignited.

Rafaello leant over her like a dark avenging hero, hot golden eyes flaming over her, primal satisfaction emanating from every hard angle of his darkly handsome features. 'And all I want to do is torture you with pleasure until you beg…'

Shock momentarily stilled the upward rise of her hips, the squirming invitation she could not prevent that close to his lean, powerful frame. Rafaello claimed a devouring kiss from her swollen lips, sending an electrifying current through her sensitised body, and gazed down at her again, connecting with the bewilderment in her passion-glazed eyes. 'And beg…and beg…until you're enslaved, *amore mia.*'

Glory tried and failed to swallow, staring up at him like a rabbit caught in car headlights, certain of destruction but hypnotised. 'S-sorry?'

Rafaello ran an expert hand down over her quivering length to the very heart of her, where she ached for the merest hint of a touch, and her entire body rose in an eager movement as unstoppable as a tidal wave. Something akin to anger burned in his intent scrutiny as he watched her respond helplessly to that provocative power-play. 'I was a bloody fool when you were eighteen. I should have taken you to bed. I don't believe that anything could have parted us then!'

'R-Rafaello…?' Glory was startled by the angry regret and bitterness that he made no attempt to hide from her.

'But we're together now, *amore*,' Rafaello growled, capturing her mouth again and shifting a hair-roughened thigh over her to hold her captive.

'I love you…' she gasped, lost in the tormenting hunger he had ignited.

Rafaello tensed and then vented a harsh laugh, scanning her with blistering golden eyes that emanated anger like a forcefield. 'If you say that *one* more time I'm walking out on you forever!'

Glory stared up at him, utterly intimidated by that threat. She could feel the tears of rejection welling up. With a roughened imprecation in Italian he curved his hands to her cheekbones and he followed the track of one salty tear with his lips in a disorientatingly tender salutation that bemused her even more. 'It's OK…' he soothed not quite levelly. 'Really, it's OK…'

All shaken up, she lay there quivering under him, scared to speak, scared to do anything in case it was the wrong thing. It was as if her whole life was up for grabs, there to be lost or gained on a single shake of the dice, for that was what *he* meant to her. In Corfu, when she had been without him, every day had stretched like an endless grey sea in front of her, empty and without colour.

He kissed her breathless and she clung to him, her own need surging higher than ever, instantly recalled, instantly reawakened. He teased the most sensitive spot in her entire body until she cried out, wanting more, driven by impulses much stronger than she was and a need that was more than she could bear. He shifted in a lithe rearrangement and employed his expert mouth on her instead.

From that point on, thought was too great a challenge and she was enslaved by her own frantic, feverish responses, her hands twisting through the thick silk of his hair, helpless cries breaking from her throat. By the time he rose over her, settled his long, muscular frame between her spread thighs, excitement had deprived her of all control. He entered her with a sure, forceful thrust and sent her spinning into a convulsive climax. Out of her senses with that sudden, shocking overload of pleasure, she cried out his name at the peak of ecstasy.

'And now you do that again, *cara*,' Rafaello instructed thickly as she came drifting back down in a sensual daze into her own body again.

'Again...' Glory echoed, 'I can't—'

'You *can*.' He surged deeper into her again, all virile male and hungry dominance. Her tender flesh was so sensitive she moaned out loud. The raw excitement snatched her up again, her heart thundering in her ears as he drove her back into the grip of pure, mindless pleasure where nothing mattered but that he not stop, where all that guided her was her own overwhelming need. And, without feeling she had anything to do with the development, she hit another shattering climax that totally wiped her out.

* * *

Glory stirred and lifted heavy eyelids to focus on the bed-side light burning at what appeared to be a very low setting.

Never quick to regain her wits on first wakening, she lost a minute or two computing the fact that she had never seen that particular lamp before. She was in Rafaello's bedroom in his penthouse apartment. The recollection of their passionate lovemaking made her face burn, but she turned cold again almost as quickly as she recalled the angry, bitter frustration he had revealed and the manner in which he had rejected her impulsive declaration of love.

Rafaello felt trapped. Of course he did. Her gabbling like some dizzy teenager about love probably made him feel even more trapped, she thought wretchedly. He might still find her attractive and he might want their baby to have a father, but that was a long way from wanting to *marry* her. But what other choice did he have? If Benito Grazzini was so keen to establish a relationship with Sam, relations between their families would have to be good and smooth. Glory's being pregnant by Rafaello and unmarried would make relations exceedingly rocky.

The sound of a door opening startled her. She rolled over to see Rafaello emerging from the bathroom. He was freshly shaven but with his hair still damp from the shower, and his sheer masculine impact took her breath away. He was already dressed in a crisp cotton shirt and dark tailored trousers. His back to her, he paused in front of a dressing mirror to fix his tie, his bold bronzed profile taut, half in shadow, half in light.

'What time is it?' she whispered.

Rafaello tensed and only half-turned to flick her a glance. 'Almost seven. I was about to wake you. Marcel is making dinner for you—'

'Marcel?'

'My chef. He'll travel down to Montague Park with you

when you decide to leave town. He has instructions that you have to eat three times a day minimum—'

Glory eased herself up slowly and clutched the sheet as if she was cold. 'Where are *you* going?'

'I have urgent business in Rome tomorrow. My life's been on hold for the past week,' Rafaello reminded her. 'Unfortunately, Grazzini Industries doesn't run itself. On the way to the airport I'll call in with Archie to announce our nuptials—'

'Our...what?' Glory could feel the distance in him again and she was super-sensitive to that rather sardonic edge to his cool drawl.

'Our wedding. I applied for the special licence this afternoon and I've booked the church down at the Park for ten days from now—'

'Ten...days?' Glory parroted in shock and then she pinned her lips shut again, for she had no desire to argue on that timing.

'The sooner we're married the better. I spoke to your father's consultant earlier as well,' Rafaello revealed, reaching for his jacket and swinging round to face her. 'By the time I get back from abroad, Archie should be up to attending our wedding in a wheelchair at least.'

'But I haven't even said I'll marry you yet...' Glory believed he ought to take note of that point and hoped it would puncture his cool.

'I rather took agreement for granted, *cara mia*.' Rafaello focused on the tumbled bedsheets with suggestive intensity before skimming his glittering dark gaze back up to her hotly flushed face. 'But, of course, if you're willing to watch World War Three break out between our families, go ahead and turn me down. This is one decision you have to make on your own.'

The silence simmered. Her tummy flipped. He was hitting her on her weakest flank. Love and hatred twinned inside her. 'You *know* I'm not going to turn you down.'

In an abrupt movement he swung away from her again, his jawline set at an aggressive angle as he made what seemed to her a quite unnecessary further adjustment to the knot on his silk tie. 'Do I?'

'Just tell me…what do you get out of marrying me?' Glory asked tightly.

'Great sex and a baby. As long as you leave the love stuff out of it,' Rafaello drawled with cutting clarity, 'I'll have no complaints.'

At that reminder, she flinched.

'Jon will be in touch with you about the wedding arrangements,' he continued. 'He'll sort out the caterers et cetera. All you have to do is buy something brilliant white and float down the aisle in it looking like an angel—'

'I can't wear white in *this* condition!'

Rafaello rested exasperated dark golden eyes on her. 'I want to see you in white…OK? Your father's a conventional man. I was planning to save the news that his first grandchild is on the way until he's feeling rather more resilient. As he's not even aware that we've been seeing each other, I should think the announcement that we're getting hitched is quite enough for the moment.'

Slowly, grudgingly she nodded in receipt of that argument. 'You have a point.'

'I also want you to move into the Park itself once you feel you can leave your father to Maud's devoted care,' Rafaello delivered.

Glory glanced at him in dismay. 'Not *before* the wedding—'

'The cottage hasn't been your home in five years, and if you can lure Sam under the same roof it might make breaking the ice between Sam and Benito easier when the time comes.'

'When is that time coming?'

'When and if Sam agrees, not before,' Rafaello told her levelly. 'My father would be over here right now if he thought Sam would be willing to meet him but he knows he has to be patient.'

And then what? But she turned her troubled thoughts back to her own problems. So, regardless of how Rafaello felt about her, she was still going to marry him, wasn't she? Coward, you spineless coward, piped up the voice of her subconscious. What he had said to her in bed, about sex on their very first date being more her style than the candlelit dinner he had romanced her over, would haunt her forever more. She shuddered. That was what Rafaello *really* thought of her. A sexy wanton with few sensibilities and even fewer morals. All right for slaking his high sex drive on, all right as an incubator for the next Grazzini but not much use for anything else.

'Well, it must give you a real kick to think that the mother of your child and your future wife is a greedy, gold-digging little tart,' Glory said grittily.

Not unnaturally, she took Rafaello entirely by surprise with that out-of-the-blue attack. He stared at her, brilliant eyes dead-level and serious. 'I *don't* think that.'

'No?' Glory widened her bright blue gaze, steeling herself to go a step further. 'Then you now accept that your precious father blackmailed me into leaving you five years ago—'

'If I thought that, I'd probably kill him,' Rafaello murmured without hesitation. 'But I don't think it or accept it, and as for the rest of it...' A rather bleak laugh fell from his lips. 'I know money's not that important to you. I got that message in Corfu.'

Reminding her that he wanted to call in with her father before he headed for the airport, he left without fanfare and she sat there, staring at the space where he had been, thinking that no matter how much she loved him she would never, ever understand what went on in that dark, complex head of his. Why did the man who was about to marry her look almost regretful when he agreed that she was not mercenary? Why did he react to the word 'love' as if it was a term of abuse?

CHAPTER NINE

'JOE thinks that finding out I'm an illegit Grazzini is on a par with winning the National Lottery!' Sam said, tight-mouthed with discomfiture.

It was Glory's first meeting with Sam since he had left London, and from the instant of his arrival she had been unsettled by her kid brother's likeness to Rafaello. The more she studied Sam, the more amazed she became that she had never once noticed the resemblance between man and boy. That black hair, those dark, deep-set, dramatic eyes. Her mother had never been that dark. The sculpted cheekbones and the newly aggressive tilt of Sam's jaw were pure Grazzini. How could she have been so blind to what was staring her in the face?

'I mean, *look* at all this stuff!' Sam spread a censorious and uneasy glance over their surroundings. They were in the rear sitting room at Montague Park, one of the less opulent rooms but still much too grand in her brother's estimation. 'Like I said to Rafaello, living like royalty is not about to go out of style with the Grazzinis around. Take that snuff box...sixty grand, and there's homeless people starving on the streets!'

Glory could not feel that Rafaello, a capitalist to the backbone, could have much enjoyed that particular lecture. 'You can knock what they've got and how they live but don't forget that Grazzini money saved Dad's life.'

'Of course, I appreciate that.' Sam kicked at the tassle fringing on a nearby chair before stuffing his equally restive hands into the pockets of his jeans and turning away. 'But I can't think of him as "Dad" any more. He said it would be OK to call him Archie if I wanted to—'

'Oh…*Sam*!' Glory was dismayed by the thought of how much that request must have hurt the older man. 'He's acted as your father for sixteen years. Isn't that worth something?'

'Yeah, but he's never loved me like he loved you. No, don't you argue about that because it's true and you can hardly blame him for feeling that way,' Sam warned her with sudden force, flipping back to face her, dark eyes full of a pain that saddened her. 'I grew up knowing I *wasn't* the son Archie Little wanted. Why do you think I play all that sport when I hate it? Only to be what *he* thought I should be. Have you any idea what it's like having it dinned into you that five generations of Littles have been gardeners here?'

Glory swallowed back impulsive words in her father's defence. Sam had to talk to someone and she was grateful that he was willing to discuss his feelings with her. Arguing with his every statement would only silence him.

Sam breathed in deep and then shrugged. 'Do you know what my first thought was when Archie told me I wasn't his kid?'

Glory shook her head.

'Thank God I don't *have* to be a gardener…can you believe I was *that* superficial?'

Glory was concealing her steadily growing shock at what she was hearing. The quiet and affectionate but always reserved eleven-year-old boy she had believed she knew so well five years earlier had turned into a young man she needed to get to know all over again.

'I was a misfit. Even Mum…' Sam muttered uncomfortably. 'Always telling me only sissies want to sit drawing pictures all the time! Narrow people with narrow minds.'

Glory paled and bit her lip. 'Sam…*please* don't talk like that—'

'You were bright enough to stay on at school and they made you leave and take a rubbish job because that was *our* place in life. Bottom of the pile and no room for ambition or imagination,' Sam shot at her with angry resentment. 'If you must know, it was a relief to find out I wasn't a Little!'

'Yes,' Glory conceded because she could truly see it had been for him. Those Grazzini genes, those strong and assertive Grazzini genes had been buzzing about below Sam's deceptively tranquil surface just waiting for the opportunity and the freedom to erupt. He was clever and he was deep and he had loathed that yoke of low expectations.

'Only problem is…' Sam gave her a rueful lopsided smile that tugged at her heartstrings. '…I'm not sure I'm up to the challenge of being even an illegit Grazzini—'

'You only need to be yourself.' Glory gave him a supportive hug and sighed. 'I love you loads, Sam. I just want you to be at peace with yourself and happy again—'

'No teenager would ever admit to being happy, Glory,' Sam mocked. 'Look, I've got a stack of work to do for my art project. Show me where I'm to kip and I'll get on with it and see you later.'

She was delighted that he was staying the night without argument. When Joe's father had dropped him off Sam had set his suitcase prominently by the front door and indicated extreme unwillingness to take up residence under the same roof as her.

Her brother followed her upstairs and then, steps slowing, he drifted away from her on the landing, drawn by the paintings lining the walls.

'Who's this?' Sam demanded, stopping dead in front of a canvas of an elderly man.

'Could be one of your ancestors…but I haven't a clue. Rafaello could tell you—'

'Yeah…but I bet this old guy was another super-achieving Grazzini,' Sam grimaced and accompanied her to the room she had selected for his hopeful occupation earlier that day. 'I'm never going to fit in anywhere, Sis.

This lot are all money mad and into big business, and I want to be an artist.'

'Why shouldn't you fit?' Glory protested. 'At least the Grazzinis appreciate art.'

Looking thoughtful at that obvious point in their favour, Sam glanced at her. 'Glad you're putting Rafaello out of his misery by marrying him.'

'How do you mean?'

'I talk to him on the phone most days,' Sam admitted. 'I still feel bad that I went for him that day in London, because once he explained how things had *been* with you two—'

'He did…what?' Glory folded her arms and surveyed her brother with a martial glint in her enquiring eyes.

'Glory…you've really given Rafaello the run-around. Be honest about it,' Sam urged. 'Of course the guy's insecure. You keep on ditching him. He's not even sure he can depend on you to show up at the church on Friday!'

'Is that a fact?' Glory absorbed this very different viewpoint of her past history with Rafaello with some difficulty.

'Why else did he suggest I should move in here if not so that if you took some crazy notion of legging it before the wedding I could warn him?'

Glory walked slowly downstairs again. Rafaello, afraid that she might get cold feet? Her susceptible heart flowered as though the sun had come out to warm it. Rafaello had been abroad for a solid week and she had left London only the evening before. He had flown from Rome to New York, where he seemed to be working eighteen-hour days. He called her most days but their conversations had been horribly impersonal. Furthermore, Rafaello had not referred to their wedding once since she had told him to mind his own business when he had asked her if she had bought a white dress. But oh, yes, Glory was eager to think that Rafaello might *care* enough about her to feel even a tiny bit insecure.

Then, as more rational thought kicked in, her face fell at dramatic speed. Of course, Rafaello *wasn't* insecure. But what a wonderfully devious and touching story he had dreamt up to persuade Sam to move even temporarily into Montague Park. Sam had until now been insisting that when he left Joe's house he wanted to return to the cottage even though it was currently empty. Yet in one easy move Rafaello had got their mutual brother beneath a Grazzini roof by lowering the macho front and asking for help and support that he didn't need!

Archie Little would not be released from hospital until the day before the wedding. Maud had stayed on in London by his side. Both her father and her future stepmother had accepted the early-retirement package that Rafaello had offered them. Not his idea either but Maud's. Rafaello had already thrown a team of workmen into a house in the village owned by the estate. A cosy home all on one floor. He was planning to sign it over to Archie and Maud when they married along with a small car. He was very generous, very thoughtful, Glory acknowledged, dashing tears from her eyes. She had to be the most spoilt woman in the world to think she could have love as well as passion, romance as well as kindness.

Here she was with a sheaf of gold credit cards, the ability to move between three different dwellings that she knew of and very possibly more, and he *was* gorgeous and she loved him to death. So what if he still believed she had sold him down the river for five thousand pounds when she was eighteen? He no longer seemed to care. And if he had been telling the truth when he had said that he would kill Benito if he believed her version of events was the correct one, well, there were enough family divisions without that development, weren't there?

Mopping her damp face with a tissue, she sat down with a maternity magazine to read articles about future motherhood that were now of absorbing interest to her. While she was scrutinising outrageously expensive but very cute items of baby apparel with dreaming eyes she heard the front door slam and then voices filtering in from the echoing hall. She stuffed the magazine behind a cushion because she was embarrassed about what had become a serious secret fix.

'*Santo cielo!*' thundered an intimidating masculine voice. 'I am Benito Grazzini. Are you trying to tell me that I am no longer welcome in my son's home?'

Glory's blood ran cold in her veins. Almost falling off the sofa in her haste, she raced over to the door to peer round it in horror. The new housekeeper, engaged by Jon Lyons, was striving to apologise and soothe. 'It's only that Mr Grazzini doesn't want Miss Little to be disturbed—'

'I'm not going to disturb her...I only want to *see* her!' Benito Grazzini growled, hoving into view like a big, burly silver-haired bear. 'Surely she's not in bed at this hour?'

Glory plastered herself up against the wall behind the door and stopped breathing. She did not even have to think about hiding—the urge came entirely naturally. So it was a further shock when the brief silence that fell was broken by yet another infinitely more familiar voice...Rafaello's, raised in anger. *Rafaello?* Where had Rafaello come from? At that moment, Glory did not care. As far as she was concerned, he was like the cavalry, riding to her rescue. She recovered the courage to peek round the door again. By that time, Rafaello and his father were exchanging staccato bursts of charged Italian in anything but a friendly way. The sight distressed her, for she knew how close they had been, and she had to intervene.

'Look...I don't know what all this is about but please stop it,' Glory pleaded anxiously, and in the abrupt silence that fell both men wheeled round to stare at her, wearing remarkably similar expressions of discomfiture. 'Sam's here and I'm sure you don't want him to hear you shouting at each other like that.'

'Are you kidding? This is as good as a soap opera. Family life in the raw, Grazzini-style!' Sam mocked from his vantage point halfway down the sweeping staircase, his attention fully lodged on the older man. But her brother was very pale, one hand gripping the bannister so tight she could see his knuckles gleaming white beneath his skin.

Sam must have been drawn by the racket. Glory almost groaned out loud, for she could not have pictured a worse way for Sam to meet his birth father for the first time.

'Just typical.' Rafaello shot his silenced parent an exasperated appraisal. 'You come in like a bull at a gate in spite of all my advice.'

'Don't be so pious. I'm finally getting a good look at my younger son for the first time in my life,' Benito said hoarsely, studying Sam where he stood with unashamed intensity and moving forward to address him direct. 'Always when I've seen you before I was afraid to stare in case I betrayed myself. I didn't even know you were here in this house. I came to talk to your sister this evening.'

Rafaello expelled his breath in an impatient hiss. 'I've already told you how I feel about that—'

'Your father can talk to me if he wants to,' Glory cut in. 'Anything's got to be better than all this bad feeling and awkwardness.'

'Yes, Rafaello.' Benito Grazzini backed her up. 'No need at all for you to fly home and come racing down here to protect Glory. We're all family now, or we will be by Friday, and we've got to mend fences as best we can. Come down and join us, Sam. But if you don't want to, that's all right too.'

'You talk even more than Rafaello does.' Sam surveyed his birth father with grudging fascination. 'It must be hard to get a word in edgeways.'

'Why do you think I shout?' Rafaello groaned, curving an arm round Glory's slight figure, and only then as he drew her back against him did she realise that she was trembling. 'Sorry, didn't know you were within hearing distance. I just didn't want Benito upsetting you, *cara.*'

One by one they all filed into the drawing room, where there was lots of space for people who might not want to be too close together. As soon as Glory had seated herself, Benito sank down on a sofa. Sam hovered way back by one of the windows and Rafaello took up what could only be described as a combative stance by the imposing fireplace. In his well-cut dark pinstripe suit, his black hair slightly tousled, his stunning eyes semi-screened by his lush black lashes above his smooth olive cheekbones, Glory really had to work hard at dredging her attention from him.

'So where and how do we start?' Benito enquired.

'I'd like to know the truth about you and Mum,' Glory told the older man, her strained gaze skimming over him fast and away again. 'She's gone and I can't ask her. But please be honest.'

'Are you out of your mind to be asking that?' Rafaello demanded.

'If I'd had the guts I'd have asked for her.' Sam sent his sister a wry glance of appreciation.

Benito squared his broad shoulders. 'Talitha and I both had what we thought were happy marriages. Then we met and discovered that there was more. She was the love of my life and with her I felt complete.'

'Are you serious?' Glory lifted her head to prompt, utterly taken aback by that speech.

The older man was watching Rafaello, whose shaken expression was revealing, and with a troubled frown he turned his attention back to Glory. 'We *did* love each other, and for a while the rest of the world just did not exist. We were very selfish and I can't pretend otherwise. When Talitha told me she was carrying my child I asked Rafaello's mother, Carina, for a divorce and perhaps only then did I appreciate how much pain I had already caused.'

'Oh...' Glory stole an anxious glance at Rafaello to see

how he was taking what appeared to be news to him as well. His father had been prepared to divorce his mother? Her heart went out to the man she loved when she saw his eyes veil and his strong bone-structure clench tight. 'I don't think we should talk about this. I was stupid even suggesting that we did—'

'No.' This time it was Rafaello who disagreed. 'I need to hear this too. I only wish I had heard the whole story three months sooner,' he told his father.

'You were too furious to listen. As I confessed to you then, Carina had a breakdown,' Benito said in weighted continuance, scrutinising the rug on the floor with fixed interest, guilt and grim regret emanating from him in waves. 'I can't even say I saw my duty then. It was Talitha who said we must finish, that we had no right to cause so much pain, that we each had children to consider…and, no matter how hard I tried to change her mind, she wouldn't see me or speak to me again.'

'Mum was like concrete when she made up her mind about anything,' Sam conceded in the strained silence that had fallen.

'You got ditched by a Little too,' Rafaello drawled in the most curious of tones, surveying his brooding parent with an air of surprise and sympathy.

'I thought you were a sleazebag who hit on my mother just for fun,' Sam told Benito in an embarrassed rush. 'But I can see it wasn't like that. You got hurt too.'

Benito rose upright and threw back his shoulders. Fixing his attention squarely on his eldest son, he said bluntly, 'Before I wear out my welcome I must admit to what I did to Glory five years ago—'

'Oh, never mind about that,' Glory broke in hastily, feeling that Rafaello had had a ghastly enough experience being forced to listen to how *his* mother, Carina, had only held on to Benito because *her* mother had ended their affair.

Rafaello pulled away from the fireplace, lean dark features taut, dark eyes glittering. '*I mind...*'

'You're getting into stuff that's nothing to do with me.' Sam spread an uneasy glance round his tense companions. 'I'll be down robbing the fridge if anyone wants me. I'm starving.'

Some of Benito's tension ebbed. 'Does Sam know?' he asked Glory.

'No, and I won't tell him.'

'You *did* threaten to sack Glory's father, didn't you?' Rafaello studied the older man with incredulous contempt. 'Glory's been telling the truth all along and you lied to me. *Why?*'

Benito grimaced. 'Your mother was still alive. I couldn't face your bringing Talitha's daughter home to meet Carina. She couldn't have coped with that. It was too close. There was the secrecy over Sam too. I was afraid of everything coming out and of Sam's home-life being wrecked...and I panicked.'

'What right did you have to visit your mistakes on *my* life?' Rafaello derided.

'None,' his father admitted heavily. 'But you and Glory had been dating such a short time, I thought that you'd soon forget each other. Obviously I was wrong on that score and probably I believed what it suited me to believe.'

'If I can't trust my own father, who *can* I trust?' Rafaello shot at him in complete disgust.

Benito was grey with strain. 'I'm sorry. I was afraid that you would turn against me if you found out about Talitha and Sam.'

As Benito walked heavily from the room Glory looked at Rafaello with pained eyes. 'Go after him. My father wasn't any keener on us dating back then. If I can forgive Benito, you can too. What are you so angry about anyway? You didn't exactly break your heart when we went our separate ways!'

'Do you think *all* Grazzinis wear their broken hearts on their sleeves?' Rafaello demanded with a bitterness that took her aback. 'My father destroyed our relationship. He lied to me about you and he threatened you...I could never forgive that!'

'Then think of Sam,' Glory told him in dismay. 'Sam relies on you and he trusts you. If you're at odds with Benito he's going to want to know why.'

'I am in no mood to overlook what we suffered through no fault of our own five years ago.' Rafaello framed each word with harsh, angry clarity. 'I *loved* you...I was devastated by what happened between us!'

Glory gazed back at him with very wide eyes. 'You...loved me? But you *smiled* at me when I said a clean break was the best idea—'

'The more I feel, the more I hide.' Brilliant dark eyes grim, Rafaello lifted his proud dark head high. 'Do you think I would have let you see that you were hurting me? You spoke as though we'd only been casual friends, behaved as though I had never meant *anything* to you—'

'I didn't know how else to behave.' Tears clogged Glory's response, for it savaged her to think that she had hurt him without even realising the fact and tore her apart to credit that he too had cared. 'I knew I loved you but we'd been together just a few weeks.'

'A few weeks was long enough. That night I delivered you home when you were sixteen, your mother actually warned me off,' Rafaello revealed, his wide sensual mouth twisting at the memory. 'As I was leaving I could not resist urging her not to be too hard on you and she saw through me—'

'Mum warned you off?' Glory exclaimed in astonishment.

'I didn't need the embargo. I didn't need to be told that you were too young for me when I had seen it for myself.

But your mother wanted to be sure that I knew that *she* knew I was interested in you even then—'

'You were thinking about me that far back...?' Glory was enchanted by that admission and she wound her fingers round his with a possessive confidence that she had never before felt with him. 'I used to hide behind trees and watch you on your motorbike. All my mates knew I was mad about you. When I saw you that night in the bar—'

'You made a real ass of yourself...but it was kind of sweet because it was all for my benefit,' Rafaello commented. 'And very funny—'

'Funny?' Glory had swallowed that first less than tactful comment but was unable to tolerate that final term.

Rafaello sent her a sudden wicked grin. 'You looked so beautiful but you hadn't a clue how to flirt and it was like watching a ten-year-old trying to be a vamp, every move wildly exaggerated—'

'It was the drink did that.' Glory's cheeks were scarlet. 'But to get back to what you were saying earlier...if you loved me when I was eighteen, why did you set me up so horribly at the restaurant that night? Letting me turn up and see you snogging that redhead—?'

'And I wouldn't have been at all surprised had you sat down at the table with us and wished me well with her,' Rafaello admitted without the remorse she had been hoping to hear. 'That was one of the worst nights of my life—'

'Well, it wasn't exactly the best night of mine!' Glory pointed out with some heat. 'And I'm still waiting for an apology because you were really cruel!'

'*I* was cruel?' Rafaello exclaimed in astonishment. 'You ditch me and then you really turn the screw by expecting me to still spend the evening with you as though absolutely *nothing* has happened?'

Glory thought about that angle and winced. 'I just wanted to spend every last possible moment with you. I didn't ditch you because I wanted to,' she reminded him.

'But I didn't *know* that. A real coward would've said no to the prospect of that evening but I was set on proving that I could be as cool and unfeeling as you appeared to be...' Rafaello hesitated, slight colour springing up over his taut cheekbones. 'So I went home and got very, very drunk. I'm a Grazzini to the backbone where love is concerned. That night I was convinced my life was *ruined*—'

Glory found his other hand, finding her hold on one was insufficient to demonstrate her need to proffer support and comfort. 'You got...drunk?'

'I arrived at the restaurant in advance of you, sat down and informed the entire table that I was planning to d-drink myself under it.' Rafaello's dark deep drawl shook with sudden amusement at the memory of that melodramatic announcement. 'So all my friends were feeling hugely sorry for me and your name was being taken very much in vain. The redhead saw you arrive and just grabbed me. I suppose she was trying to help me save face—'

'Rafaello,' Glory muttered shakily, her hands releasing his fingers to work up his sleeves in little comforting squeezes. 'I was stupid. Because I didn't know you cared, I didn't realize what I was putting you through. I can't bear to think I hurt you—'

'But I got healthily furious when Benito told me about the five grand a couple of days later.' Rafaello gazed down at her with lustrous dark golden eyes that made her heart skip a beat. 'And of course my father's lies ensured that I wasn't tempted to go after you—'

'I just can't believe that you loved me then.' Her lovely face mirroring the strength of her regret, Glory released an unhappy sigh. 'In fact, I just can't bear that you loved me and we *still* lost each other—'

Linking her caressing fingers round his neck, Rafaello backed her down onto the sofa. 'It makes a big difference to me that you didn't throw up what we had by choice, although I still don't understand why you didn't just tell me what Benito was threatening to do.'

'I didn't have enough confidence to do that. It seemed to me that, no matter what happened, it would be my family that suffered, so it seemed wiser just to keep quiet. I love your eyes...' Glory confided, her mind travelling off in another direction entirely as he rearranged her against the cushions. She was blissfully lost in the smouldering dark golden depths trained on her with hungry but tender intensity. 'We're going to be married in forty-eight hours and I can't wait—'

Rafaello stilled as though something in that reference to time had ensnared him, and then he froze and levered himself back from her. '*Dio mio*...what am I *doing*?'

'Nothing I don't want you to do,' Glory was quick to assert, slim fingers closing round the parted edges of his suit jacket as she attempted to ease him back to her.

Rafaello surveyed her beautiful expectant face and the inviting curve of her pink mouth and groaned out loud in frustration. 'I have to fly straight back to New York—'

'*What?*' Glory sat up fast and linked imprisoning hands round his neck, fingers spearing into the thick black silk of his hair.

'This was a literal flying visit, *cara mia*. I only came over because I realised my father was set on approaching you this evening and I knew you were scared of him—'

'Not any more...don't go,' she begged.

'I have to.' He drew her hands down, pressed a fervid kiss of regret to one of her palms and then sprang upright again. 'We've got Sam in the house too. We really can't consider cavorting on a sofa like randy teenagers—'

'No...' she agreed in some embarrassment at that reminder, but her voice wobbled, for she could not stand letting him go.

Rafaello made it to the door and then he swung round, hauled her into his arms and claimed a passionate kiss which sent her temperature rocketing. 'Forty-eight hours…' he reminded her raggedly, pulling away again and backing across the hall in the general direction of the front door, not removing his attention from her for a second.

'Are you all right?' Glory gasped as he banged his shoulder off the edge of the marble hall fireplace.

'Aching more in places I wouldn't like to mention, *bella mia*,' Rafaello groaned.

He departed and she went off in search of Sam, but the kitchen was in darkness. Only when she went back up to the ground floor again did she hear her brother laughing.

Closer investigation revealed that Sam was in the games room. Benito had not departed as she had assumed. His jacket doffed and a cue in one hand, he was instructing Sam in the noble art of billiards. After a covert glance in at father and son getting on so well, she tiptoed away again, leaving them in peace.

Well, she told herself dizzily, Rafaello had been in love with her when she was eighteen and that was really encouraging to find out. What he had managed once he could, with careful encouragement, manage again. Now that she had time to think about it, she was even more heartened by his admission that he had been devastated when they broke up back then. He had cared, *really* cared about her after just six weeks…and no sex. Maybe if she had contrived to stay out of his bed in Corfu for more than an hour after her arrival she might have reanimated those warmer feelings.

So, in retrospect, even though she would have been very willing to make love on the sofa, she was frantically grateful that the demands of business had made that impossible. Maybe resisting him was the secret, maybe he needed a challenge, only it was rather difficult to work out how she could meet that expectation once they were married…

CHAPTER TEN

THE next two days were incredibly busy for Glory. She tidied and aired the cottage for her father's return from hospital. She visited the vicar who was to conduct the service, enjoyed half a dozen lengthy visits from former schoolfriends, who were surprised and delighted at their receipt of wedding invitations, and finally she welcomed her father home.

'Sam's taken to Benito Grazzini, then,' Archie Little gathered within ten minutes of his return, having learned that Rafaello's father was still staying at the Park.

'Does it bother you?' Glory asked awkwardly.

'It's only what I expected. Sam's been one of them from birth,' the older man remarked with a wry smile of acceptance. 'I tried to make him into a Little, goodness knows I did, but even as a little kid he had all his own ideas. But it's not his fault he was a cuckoo in the nest.'

He was a practical man and she supposed it was just as well, for there was already talk of Sam going over to Benito's home in Tuscany for his half-term break, and Benito was talking about the possibility of buying a house in London. For the foreseeable future, Sam was going to be dividing his time between two families and two very different lifestyles.

Rafaello got back to Montague Park on the night before the wedding. He was not overjoyed to discover that Glory was spending her last night of singledom at the cottage and much, much too busy even to see him. 'See you at the altar!' she told him cheerfully on the phone.

'I just want to see you for five minutes—'

'No, I'm sorry. I promised Dad I would devote myself

to him tonight and if I see you, well, you *know* it's not going to be for just five minutes.'

Ten minutes later, the knocker on the cottage door went. Rafaello was on the doorstep.

'Wedding gift,' Rafaello drawled, shoving a slim parcel into her startled hands.

'Oh...oh—er—thanks!' she exclaimed in surprise, momentarily deflected from literally eating him up with her eyes.

'Engagement ring.' Rafaello settled a small box on top of the first package and then a second box as well. 'Eternity ring—felt I might as well get it all over with at once,' he imparted as he met her astonished gaze.

Glory thrust the gifts on the dresser to one side of the door and was just within an ace of throwing herself exuberantly into his arms when he backed off in an exaggerated step, both lean hands rising as if to hold her at bay.

'I can play hard to get too, *bella mia*.' A sizzling smile slanted his darkly handsome features, his stunning eyes full of pure gold mockery. '*Buona notte!*'

And with that he sauntered back to his red Ferrari, all fluid grace, cool and extreme sexiness.

Lacking that subtle touch, Glory raced down the path in his wake. 'You can come in if you like—'

Rafaello paused with one hand on the open door of his car and skimmed her a glance of vibrant amusement and satisfaction. 'I wouldn't dream of it. I almost forgot...' he murmured smoothly. 'Don't be late at the church. It's two minutes away and I will just come and fetch you—'

'It's tradition for the bride to be a little late!'

'Stuff tradition,' Rafaello enunciated, springing into the Ferrari. 'I want you there on the stroke of the hour.'

Glory shot between him and the car door and yanked his keys out of the ignition. 'OK...what's going on?' she asked anxiously because, although she was charmed by his wonderfully light-hearted mood, she was disconcerted by the alteration she sensed in him.

'What's going *on*?' Rafaello laughed. 'I'm just happy!'

'Oh…' As that was news that could only please any woman the night before their wedding, Glory returned his car keys to him.

But Rafaello climbed out of the car, pushed shut the door and lounged back against it. He breathed in very deep. 'I'm happy because when we were in London you told me you loved me and I'm hoping like hell that you meant it…'

Taken aback by that blunt admission, Glory reddened. 'Of course I meant it.'

His brilliant eyes gleamed and he startled her by snatching her up off her feet, striding round the bonnet and stowing her in his passenger seat.

'For goodness' sake, what are you doing?' Glory yelped.

'I'm kidnapping you,' Rafaello asserted, swinging in beside her and firing the engine before she could do anything about it.

'Are you crazy? I was about to make Dad's supper—'

Having accelerated back down onto the lane, Rafaello jammed on his brakes and lifted his car phone to stab out a number. 'Sam? Yes, I told her I was kidnapping her but she's not impressed by the dramatic gesture—she's more concerned about Archie's supper—'

Glory's cheeks flamed at that proclamation. Rafaello replaced the phone and dealt her an amused appraisal. 'Sam will ensure that your father eats…OK? Can you relax now?'

It was a beautiful early-autumn evening. He parked the Ferrari below the beech trees that lined the woodland walk that followed the river through the estate. Closing a lean hand round hers, he tugged her out of the car. 'I had to talk to you before the wedding, *bella mia*.'

'What wouldn't keep until tomorrow?' Glory teased.

Rafaello came to a halt. 'It crossed my mind on the flight

back home that although you had heard me telling Sam that I loved you, I had never actually told you…at least, nor properly.'

'Not properly…' Glory repeated unsteadily, her attention resting on the decided colour that had risen to accentuate his fabulous cheekbones. 'Are you trying to say that you were serious when you said that to Sam in London? I thought you were just saying it to calm him down—'

'I'm not that good a liar in moments of crisis where you're concerned. If you hadn't done a runner on me in Corfu I would have told you I loved you then.'

Glory was desperate to believe that he loved her but afraid to credit that what she most wanted could already be hers. 'But that last morning we were together at the villa you were so grim and tense with me…that's why I got the idea that you were going to dump me!' Glory explained awkwardly. 'I don't want you feeling you have to rewrite history just because I got pregnant and you want to make me feel better about our getting married.'

His lean strong face clenched hard with tension. 'I don't believe this. I've never told a woman I loved her in my life, and the minute I do you start telling me I *don't*! But then, how can I blame you for that when I've made such a hash of everything? I *always* get it wrong with you—'

Colliding with the raw emotion in his lustrous dark eyes, Glory started really listening instead of doubting. 'You don't—'

'Yes, I do. Even when you told me that you loved me, I screwed up!' Rafaello ground out, swinging away from her and raking his fingers through his black hair in a movement of violent frustration. 'I thought you were only saying it because you had guessed that I was crazy about you and you were feeling sorry for me. That stung my pride—'

Dumbfounded by the revelation that Rafaello could be that insecure, Glory closed her hands round one lean clenched fist and drew him back to her again, but he was so busy talking, he hardly seemed to notice. 'There's *never* been anyone else for me but you,' he was telling her aggressively. 'When I first saw you again I went haywire and came up with the mistress idea. I just wanted you back on any terms I could have you without losing face.'

As Rafaello paused for breath Glory was starting to smile. 'Without losing face?' she encouraged.

'Then I wrecked things again by coming off with that rubbish about you trying to trap me by getting pregnant,' Rafaello informed her with a guilty grimace. 'I was in shock at finding out you were still a virgin, but by the time I got out of the shower I had actually quite warmed up to the idea that you might conceive my child—'

'You...*had*?'

'Then I realised you'd gone out in the storm, and I don't *ever* want to relive that panic you put me in, *cara*,' Rafaello confided with a positive shudder of recollection. 'By the time I got you back up to the villa, I knew I had much deeper feelings for you than I had been prepared to admit—'

'So you proposed marriage to me when I was in the bath. Trouble is, I didn't think you meant it—'

'I'm not like my father. I was really impressed listening to him giving forth about your mother and without a shred of self-consciousness admitting that she was the love of his life. I'm just not great with the words,' Rafaello interrupted with raw regret, strained dark eyes holding hers as if he was willing her with every atom of his being to believe in him. 'But I just looked at you and my feelings...well, they just *overwhelmed* me and I know it wasn't the most romantic proposal *or* the best place to propose—'

Glory was so shaken by that disjointed burst of confidence that her eyes stung with tears. 'And I rejected the idea straight off. I'm so sorry I didn't listen—'

'No, it was my fault, throwing it at you like that,' Rafaello insisted, gathering her close and snatching in a sustaining breath. 'I realised that I had to try to prove to you that we could be happy together—'

'You succeeded—'

'But I didn't have the guts to sit down and trash the mistress arrangement straight off in case you just upped and walked out there and then,' Rafaello confessed in a charged undertone of embarrassment. 'Then that last night we had that stupid argument and you said how mortified you'd be if your family knew what you were doing with me…I honestly thought you despised me for being such a jerk—'

All those brains, Glory reflected in silent fascination, and he could not see the wood from the trees when it came to her feelings for him. 'I was just saying that because I was angry with you—'

'But I felt so guilty and ashamed. Then when I came to bed thinking you would be asleep, you turned out to be awake,' he reminded her. 'And I was dreading saying what I knew I *had* to say…'

'Which was?' Glory prompted.

'That I was sorry that I had forced you into becoming my mistress but that I had never once thought of you that way because I loved you and still wanted to marry you—'

'Why on earth were you *dreading* saying that to me?' Glory demanded in some bewilderment.

Shimmering golden eyes assailed hers in a head-on collision and his hard jawline clenched. 'I was scared you would just pack your bags and go—'

'But I was nuts about you too!' Glory exclaimed. 'I suppose you were so tense the next morning because you were *still* thinking that but, you see, I thought you were warming up to dumping me. How on earth could you think I would walk out on you after the way I'd behaved in bed with you?'

'Passion didn't mean you wouldn't grab the first chance you got to have your freedom back.'

'I hope you know different now. Passion and love go together for me,' Glory informed him gently.

'When I got back and found you gone I was shattered,' Rafaello muttered heavily. 'I assumed you'd gone back to England and I hired an investigation agency to search for you—'

'You...*did*?' Glory was shocked by that admission.

'Then your father fell ill and I was finally able to find you after two months of hell—'

'But you were so distant—'

'Even the most stupid guy would get the message that he was unwanted after being ditched twice over, *bella mia*,' Rafaello pointed out defensively. 'And the way you kept on thanking me all the time for doing what I could for Archie made me feel even worse. I was also feeling very uncomfortable with the fact that *I* knew Sam was my brother but *you* didn't.'

Glory's bright blue eyes shone like stars as she gazed up at him. 'You never have been unwanted by me in your entire life, Rafaello Grazzini,' she swore with a slight break in her voice. 'You love me, you *really* love me—?'

'So much I can't keep my hands off you in public places.' Registering that he was on a decided winning streak, Rafaello hauled her even closer and kissed her with hungry passion, breathing raggedly in the aftermath. 'I can't wait to marry you, I just can't wait...'

They didn't stay out long. He took her home and they parted and Glory went indoors and gave her brother a big hug. 'You're even cleverer than I thought you were,' she told him.

Sam laughed but he was bewildered. 'Why?'

'Sorry, can't explain. But you were right about something that I am incredibly happy to have been *wrong* about,' his sister said with an ecstatic smile that left him none the wiser.

It was her father who reminded her about the gifts which

Rafaello had brought. Glory discovered that the slim parcel contained a jewel-case which contained an exquisite diamond and platinum necklace and drop earrings. She was overwhelmed by Rafaello's generosity but it all meant so much more to her now that she knew she was loved. Her engagement ring, the gift which most touched her heart, was an equally beautiful diamond solitaire, and the eternity ring, a narrow matching band.

The next morning, the day of the wedding, she was up early and had only just gone upstairs when she heard a car pulling up outside. Maud, who had come over to help her get dressed, called up to tell her that she had a visitor.

Glory was disconcerted to be told that Rafaello's father was waiting to speak to her. Maud had shown him into the rarely used front parlour. The reason for Benito Grazzini's visit shook Glory even more. He had come to give her a very beautiful diamond tiara that had belonged to his own mother.

'I always planned to give this to Rafaello's bride but it took me until this morning to work up the courage to offer it to you,' Benito admitted anxiously. 'I very much want to repair the damage I have done to you and to Rafaello and I also wish to welcome you with a whole heart to our family.'

Recognising the depth of the older man's sincerity, Glory thanked him and told him that she had already forgiven him and that Rafaello would soon feel the same.

Maud exclaimed over the tiara but was even more impressed by Rafaello's gifts. 'He's certainly pushed the boat out and no mistake!'

'It's just so extravagant...all this for me.' Glory fingered the gorgeous necklace with reverent fingers. 'It's like a dream.'

'Just like a wedding ought to be,' the older woman said with warm approval.

An hour or more later, when Glory studied her reflection

in the mirror, a glow of incredible happiness consumed her. The instant she had seen the dress in an exclusive wedding store in London she had fallen madly in love with it. The neckline was off the shoulder and elegant and the intricate bodice of silver beaded and embroidered silk ended in a flattering V-waistline. The sleeves were tight but flared out into a fall of exquisite lace at the elbow. The satin-silk skirt opened at the centre to reveal a panel of the same gorgeous beaded silk as the bodice. Having set aside the pretty fake tiara she had intended to wear with her Chantilly lace bridal veil, she had replaced it with the diamond tiara that Benito had given her.

Glory went downstairs to join her father, Maud having already left for the church. Leaning on the stick that gave him the extra support he needed while he was still slightly unsteady on his feet, the older man looked very well. But as she reached the hall Glory's brow indented. 'What's that noise? It sounds like horses…'

'Strewth…' Archie Little gasped in astonishment at the sight that met his eyes when he peered out of the front door.

Rafaello had sent not a car to collect her and her father but an open carriage lined in sapphire velvet, driven by a coachman in a full regalia and pulled by four white horses ornamented with elaborate plumes. Glory was thrilled to bits.

'The boy's certainly doing you proud,' was all her shaken father could think to comment when a wildly impractical white carpet was unrolled to pave her entry into the church.

Glory alighted on the white carpet and smiled for the photographers and floated along the carpet into the church and down the aisle to join Rafaello at the altar in a blissful daze.

'You look like a fairytale princess,' he whispered, shimmering golden eyes riveted to her in heart-stopping admiration. 'Just as I always imagined, *bella mia*.'

After the marriage service they travelled back in the carriage to Montague Park, where the wedding breakfast was to be served. The ballroom had been transformed with glorious flower arrangements into the most magnificent backdrop for the occasion. In the afternoon the bride and groom departed, but not before Glory had thrown her bouquet and her future stepmother had caught it.

They were to spend their honeymoon in the Grazzini home in Tuscany. Arriving there at dusk, Rafaello carried her over the threshold and straight upstairs to a gorgeous bedroom, where he finally got his bride into his arms without an audience.

'I have had the most wonderful day,' Glory informed him, gazing up at him with shining eyes of love and contentment.

'It's been the happiest day of my life, *amore mia*.' Rafaello framed her lovely smiling face with possessive fingers, studying her with passionate tenderness. 'And, if I have anything to do with it, *every* day you spend with me will be the same...'

Just over a year later Glory tucked their infant son into his cot. At almost six months old, Lorenzo had silky black curls and big blue eyes. He was a friendly, cheerful baby with a wonderful smile who slept well, ate well and loved being cuddled.

They had flown out to the villa in Corfu only that afternoon. The night before, they had celebrated the first anniversary of their marriage with a special family dinner at Montague Park. Glory was thinking how happy she had been to have her father and Maud, Sam and Benito all at the same table with nobody seeming to feel the slightest bit awkward any more. The divisions between their families had been healed and Rafaello had long since regained his former closeness with his father.

Archie and Maud had got married a couple of months after Glory and Rafaello and had then surprised everyone by taking over the village shop and embarking on a pretty busy lifestyle which seemed to suit them very well. Sam had lived with them in their new home in the village until he completed his school year and was able to sit his exams. He had then spent most of the summer in Tuscany with Benito and had returned with a good grasp of Italian. Determined to stay in advance of her kid brother, Glory had started taking lessons to learn the same language faster. Sam was currently studying for his A levels at a London school and he spent regular weekends with Archie and Maud. Benito had bought a city apartment, where Sam had come to grudging terms with living in the lap of luxury, but only after being made to appreciate how much the Grazzinis gave to charitable causes.

Glory had enjoyed a blissfully happy first year of marriage. She still wondered why it had taken her such a very long time to realise that Rafaello adored her. He had shown her his love in Corfu those first weeks they had been together, shown her in so many ways while her father was ill, but her own low self-esteem had blinded her to what she was seeing. In the same way, the strength of her love had enabled her to respect the sacrifice her mother had made in giving up Rafaello's father for the sake of their respective families. And she finally understood all the harshly offered moral principles which her parent had endeavoured to instil in her daughter. Giving way to her own passion for Benito Grazzini had ultimately caused Talitha Little great unhappiness, and she had undoubtedly wanted to protect Glory from making a similar mistake.

'Lorenzo's not asleep *already*, is he?' Rafaello demanded in disappointment as he strode into the nursery and sprang Glory from her thoughts.

She watched her tall, dark and undeniably gorgeous husband stare down ruefully into the cot where his baby son was indeed sound asleep, long lashes lying smooth on his peaceful little face.

'You were on the phone to Benito for ages,' Glory reminded him.

'I don't get enough time to play with our son,' Rafaello lamented. 'He's out like a light every night by eight. I thought babies were supposed to be night owls—'

'We don't *want* him to be a night owl,' Glory assured her husband, trying not to laugh at the tenor of his complaint. 'I don't think you'd be too pleased if he was crying in the middle of the night.'

Rafaello processed that alternative option and gave her a sizzling smile of comprehension that warmed her cheeks. 'As always where our son is concerned, you are right, *bella mia*. Such a shame that you never got to use all that knowledge you acquired reading at least a thousand magazines on what to do with a crying baby. By the end of our honeymoon, I knew more about babies than ninety-nine out of a hundred first-time fathers-to-be and we had hit every baby shop in Tuscany at least twice—'

'Stop teasing me,' Glory warned him, rather embarrassed by the reminder of how obsessive she had been in those pursuits during her pregnancy. 'Why were you on the phone so long to your father?'

'Benito has volunteered to become chairman of a charity for the homeless—'

Glory struggled not to smile. Sam's social conscience had evidently stretched to enclose his birth father. 'That's good news, isn't it?'

'Yes. He has too much energy to settle into full-time retirement and he has a huge number of contacts to offer.' Rafaello reached out to bring her slim body into connection with his big powerful frame, his mouth curving with satisfaction as she gave a faint little quiver of response.

Dio mio, cara mia…' he breathed huskily, lustrous dark golden eyes gleaming over with a wealth of tender appreciation and warmth. 'How come you married a guy who tied himself up in knots just trying to tell you that he loved you?'

'I had high hopes of how he would turn out,' Glory teased, stretching her arms up to link them round his neck, looking up into his darkly handsome features with an accelerating heartbeat and the sensation that she was one of the luckiest women in the world. 'You can actually say, "I love you" without blushing like mad now!'

'Are you ever going to let me forget that?' Rafaello groaned.

'No chance…' It was one of Glory's most tender memories. His love was all that more special and precious because he had never said those words to anyone but her. That one small fact alone made up for the years they had spent apart.

'I adore you, *bella mia*,' he murmured, his stunning eyes telegraphing the same message into hers and making her melt inside and out. 'I think you're a wonderful wife and a fabulous mother and the most incredibly loving and sexy woman alive—'

'I love you too,' Glory told him breathlessly, and while Lorenzo slept on in perfect tranquillity his parents kissed and exchanged mutual compliments which grew increasingly excessive in nature. Eventually, Rafaello swept Glory off into their bedroom next door where they sealed their love with the passion that never failed to fill them both with renewed joy and contentment.

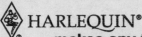

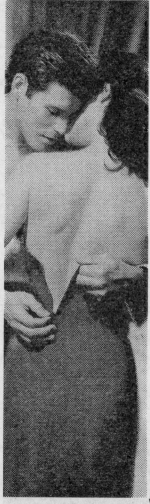